"You wan[...] pregnan[...] own up [...] am.

Rufus received the news with a moment or two of silence. "Strange, isn't it?" he said at last. "I tried for two years to father a child with Claire and failed—"

"But just one encounter with me and bingo!" said Jo bitterly.

Rufus took her hands. "So let's discuss what happens next."

She frowned. "What do you mean? Nothing happens next. Not until May of next year."

His grasp tightened. "You obviously haven't thought this through. Look, Jo…all I can do is try to put things right—"

"Don't dare offer me money," she interrupted fiercely.

"I'm offering something quite different. As I said before, I would very much like a child. And I would prefer that child to have a father married to his mother. Are you with me so far, Jo?"

Dear Reader,

Pennington, my favorite location, is my own creation. Having lived in the past near two attractive towns in the heart of England, I combine the best features of both, not least the picturesque buildings from olden times. My fictional town has wide streets, quaint tearooms and public gardens ablaze with flowers; there are irresistible shops with elegant clothes and jewelery, while others are filled with bargains in antique furniture and porcelain. Surrounded by lush countryside, Pennington is full of charm—a place where dreams come true.

Sincerely,

Catherine George

P. S. Look out for more stories from Pennington in Harlequin Romance!

The Second Bride
Catherine George

Harlequin Books

TORONTO • NEW YORK • LONDON
AMSTERDAM • PARIS • SYDNEY • HAMBURG
STOCKHOLM • ATHENS • TOKYO • MILAN
MADRID • WARSAW • BUDAPEST • AUCKLAND

ISBN 0-373-03449-0

THE SECOND BRIDE

First North American Publication 1997.

Printed in U.S.A.

CHAPTER ONE

TORRENTIAL rain had slowed to a steady downpour as the storm receded, grumbling, leaving a power cut as its parting shot. As the taxi drove away Jo hurried up the path in total darkness, then stopped halfway, listening. Someone was following her. She swung round belligerently.

'Who's there?' she demanded.

A flash of lightning lit up a hard, masculine face above a glimmer of pale raincoat before darkness fell again.

'*You?*' she said incredulously.

'Good evening, Jo,' said Rufus Grierson. 'Sorry to startle you. I waited for you in the car.'

She breathed in shakily. '*Why?* It's after midnight. Is something wrong?'

'No more than usual. Could I come in for a minute?'

Jo peered at his tall shape through the darkness while her heartbeat slowed. 'Well—yes I suppose so.' She fumbled in her bag for her key. 'But you'll have to find your way up to the top floor in the dark.'

'This must keep you fit,' he observed, close behind her as she led the way up several flights of stairs, his manner as laconic and impersonal as the last time they'd spoken, almost a year before.

'Not so you'd notice,' panted Jo, out of breath for

reasons other than exertion as they reached her door. 'I'll go in first and find a torch. Wait here, please.'

Leaving her unexpected visitor on the landing, Jo felt her way through her sitting room to the kitchen area, her hands trembling as she searched in a drawer for a torch. Thankful it was still working, she found her meagre supply of candles, stuck them on saucers and distributed flickering lights round the room. She beckoned Rufus inside, and he closed the door behind him, standing just inside the confines of the attic flat that Jo called home.

'You'd better take off your raincoat,' she said awkwardly, removing her own. 'I'll put it in the bathroom to drip.'

'Thank you,' said Rufus Grierson. He handed the expensive garment over and ran a hand through his wet hair. 'It's later than I thought. I apologise. I lost track of the time.'

Jo took the coats away and hung them up in her tiny bathroom, feeling utterly shattered by Rufus Grierson's presence in her flat. For some time now she'd been sure that their last meeting, almost a year ago, had been just that—the last time they would ever meet, unless by accident. At first she'd hoped— longed—to hear from him, but as the months went by she'd gradually resigned herself to the fact that Rufus thought of her merely as a painful reminder of all he'd lost. Yet now he was here, out of the blue. Why? Jo pulled herself together and rejoined him.

'Do sit down,' she said politely. 'Coffee?'

Rufus sat on her sofa and crossed his long legs. 'Could you possibly run to something stronger?'

Jo nodded, and, torch in hand, went to the kitchen for the bottle of brandy her mother insisted on for emergencies. Jo collected two glasses, went back to her guest and asked him to pour.

'Thank you,' said Rufus. 'I take it you're having some too?'

'Just a little.' Hoping it would calm her down, she took the glass from him and sat in her usual chair. 'Stupid of me to offer coffee with no electricity to make it.'

'It seemed impolite to point that out.' He poured an equally sparing measure for himself, but left the brandy untouched beside him. He sat looking at Jo in silence, his face haggard in the flickering candlelight, with new lines carved in it since she'd last seen him. At last she could stand it no longer, and asked him bluntly why he was actually here in her flat long past a socially acceptable time for a visit.

'I was in the Mitre earlier for a meal with a colleague,' he said obliquely. 'I saw you behind the bar in the other room, but you were run off your feet. There was obviously no chance of talking to you there, so I drove round here later and waited for you to come home.'

'I might not have been coming home,' she pointed out. 'Or I could have moved.'

'I did some research on both points first, naturally.'

'I see,' said Jo. Not that she did.

'Do you know what day it is?' he asked.

Did he think she could have forgotten? She stared blindly into her glass. 'It's your wedding anniversary.'

'You remembered, then.'

Her chin went up. 'Of course I remembered.'

'I thought you might. Bridesmaids usually do.'
Rufus Grierson gazed at her through the dim, flickering light, his brooding eyes dark in the olive-skinned
face which always, to Jo, wore a look of superiority,
as though Rufus considered himself a cut above her.
Jo Fielding and Rufus Grierson had never been
comfortable in each other's vicinity. Which had been
awkward when he married her closest friend, Claire.

'How are you?' asked Jo after a long, difficult
pause.

'I get by,' he said very quietly. 'And you?'

'The same. I work hard.'

'Does it help?'

'Yes.' She looked at him squarely. 'Tell me, after
all this time why exactly are you here, Rufus? On this
day, of all days, I must be the last person you want
to see.'

'On the contrary.' He drank some of his brandy.
'Though I admit I deliberately arranged a business
dinner for tonight with someone who had never met
Claire, in an effort to avoid talking about her.' He
paused, jaw set. 'It still hurts.'

Jo had no doubt of it.

'Then I caught sight of you behind the bar,' Rufus
went on, 'and suddenly I *needed* to talk about Claire.
And who better to talk to on this subject than you!
So when the man left I drove round here.'

'Just to talk about Claire?' Jo stared at him sus-
piciously. 'But you always resented me—and the time
she spent with me.'

'Actually, you're mistaken. I didn't resent it at all.'
He glanced at the candle on the table behind him.
'This is on its last legs. Do you have any more?'

'Afraid not.'

'Could you borrow some from the other tenants?'

'Everyone's away,' admitted Jo with some reluctance. 'We'll have to make do with these.'

'Then put a couple out and save them for later.'

Jo got up and extinguished two of the candles, plunging the room into semi-darkness. She felt light-headed, both with fatigue and the shock of meeting Rufus again. It was hard to grapple with the fact that she was alone in a room with the man Claire had wanted for a husband from the moment she first set eyes on him. Rufus had been the perfect husband for Claire, just what the Beaumonts had always dreamed of for their daughter—successful, secure, even attractive, in a remote, damn-your-eyes kind of way.

But Rufus Grierson, thought Jo bitterly, had never approved of his wife's closest friend. A freelance journalist who spent evenings behind a bar to make ends meet had rather obviously been a bit hard to take for the successful, ultra-conventional lawyer. Jo, determinedly cool in return, had kept her own opinion of him secret from Claire and made sure their paths crossed as little as possible. For Claire's sake the husband and the friend had preserved the civilities. And once Claire was dead Rufus Grierson had obviously seen no reason to come into contact with Jo Fielding again. Until now. Tonight was their first encounter since the funeral, and to her dismay Jo felt no more at ease in his presence now than she had then.

'You want me to go,' Rufus read her mind.

'No,' she said quickly. 'If it helps you to stay for a while, please do. Talk about Claire as much as you like. When I visit her parents they talk about nothing else, of course, which is—painful.' Jo bit a suddenly quivering bottom lip. 'It's different with my own family. When Claire's name comes up we just chat about her normally.'

'It's good that you can do that. Claire enjoyed spending time with your family—probably because it was so different from her own.' His eyes shadowed. 'She was a much indulged only child, of course. Growing up must have been a lot different for you, Jo. Tell me about it.'

She eyed him doubtfully. 'Are you sure you want to know? Our household bore no resemblance at all to the Beaumonts'.'

Rufus smiled faintly. 'So I gathered from Claire. I was always curious about the attraction it held for her.'

'Contrast, I suppose. There was never much cash to spare in my family, but the atmosphere at home was always—well, happy, really. My father taught classics at Pennington Boys School and coached the first-eleven cricket team. Even when he was at home he usually had some pupil or other around for extra tuition. Dad was a darling, but a typical academic— not the least handy about the house. There was no money to pay people to do the decorating, so my mother did it all, in between her PPP work—'

'What on earth was that?' he asked, relaxing slightly.

'Painting pet portraits,' Jo informed him. 'She always seemed to have a paintbrush in her hand for one reason or another, not to mention a hammer, or a screwdriver. She was perpetually mending some-thing—in between baking and making our clothes and doing the gardening and helping us with homework and so on.'

'Is she still alive?'

'Very much so! My sister Thalia lives in part of one of those large country houses they divide up into posh apartments, and Mother lives in the lodge at one of the gates.' Jo smiled a little. 'She doesn't have to do repairs any more but she still paints animal portraits. My other sister lives only a few miles from her in Oxford, too, so it suits everyone.'

'I heard that your father died.'

'Yes.' Jo's smile vanished. 'I miss him. It was hard to lose him so soon after—' She sipped some of her brandy hastily, coughed for a moment, then looked at him diffidently. 'It was good of you to write to Mother. She moved not long afterwards. But that's enough about my family. You really wanted to talk about Claire.'

'Not exclusively. I think I just needed to talk to someone who loved Claire for what she was—not a saint, but a warm, loving human being. Her parents have totally canonised her since she died.' Rufus drained his glass. 'May I have another drink?' he added, the diminishing light giving his voice a curiously disembodied quality.

'Of course.'

He poured a little brandy into his glass. 'I've sold the house at last.'

'Perhaps that's a good thing.'

'It is. I should have done it right away. It was so full of Claire, I had no hope of coming to terms with her death while I stayed there. I kept expecting to hear her voice, see her walk through the door.' Eyes sombre, he sipped some of his drink. 'So I moved into town. I've spent a lot of time packing and unpacking tea chests lately. I found these. I thought you'd like to have them as a keepsake.' Rufus took a small jeweller's box from his pocket and snapped it open.

Jo felt a searing pang of pain as she stared at the pendent pearl earrings that Claire had worn on her wedding day. She shook her head involuntarily. 'I— I can't take these, Rufus. They should go to Mrs Beaumont.'

'I handed the rest of Claire's jewellery over after the funeral,' he said quietly. 'I'd rather you had the pearls. I'm sure Claire would too. They were my personal wedding present to her, if you remember.'

Jo nodded wordlessly. How could she forget? Claire's wedding day was imprinted indelibly on her mind.

Rufus took a deep, ragged breath. 'I came across an old dinner jacket the other day and found the earrings in the pocket. Claire must have taken them off when we were at some party or other.' He held them out. 'She would have wanted you to have them.'

Jo took the box reluctantly. 'Thank you. I'll— treasure them.' But she would never wear them. Gypsy hoops were more her style.

There was an awkward pause while they avoided each other's eyes, Rufus sitting like a graven image.

'Are you still writing?' he asked at last.

'Yes. I'm just finishing a novel.' Now, why on earth had she told him *that*?

'A novel?'

'Yes.' Jo peered at him through the gloom. 'Did you think I gave up my job at the *Gazette* because I was allergic to steady employment?' She forced a shaky little laugh, trying to lighten the atmosphere. 'Ah! You did.'

'Of course not. But Claire never mentioned a novel.'

'I didn't tell her.' Jo hesitated. 'I wanted to find out if I could do it before broadcasting the news. Mother knows what I'm up to, of course, but no one else. Except you now.' She eyed him militantly.

'Your secret's safe with me.'

'No one you know would be remotely interested, anyway,' she retorted.

'So you work at the Mitre instead of starving in a garret,' Rufus remarked, making a visible effort to shrug off his melancholy. 'Do you earn enough to make life bearable?'

'Oh, yes,' she assured him. 'My articles pay reasonably well. My father left me a tiny legacy from an insurance policy, which eased my path quite a bit, and when Mother sold the house here in Pennington she gave me a bit more. It ran to a very basic word processor, and left me something in the bank for emergencies.' She paused, flushing, suddenly aware that she was talking too much. 'How about you, Rufus?'

'Like you, my work fills the vacuum. The firm's busy as ever, due to the solid client base we've established over the past few years. My brother's joined it now.'

'I don't know much about law. Do you specialise?'

He nodded. 'I advise merchant banks, financial in-stitutions, public limited companies—that kind of thing.'

'Sounds very high-powered.'

'It keeps me busy.'

There was silence for a moment, then Jo got up and relit one of the candles. 'I wish the electricity would come back. Silly, really, but the moment we get a power cut I yearn for tea.'

'It's human nature to yearn for what we can't have,' said Rufus, with sudden, startling bitterness.

Jo felt a lump in her throat. The first wedding anniversary after his wife's death was obviously hard for him. She sat down again, peering at the taut, hard features she could only just make out in the gloom. 'I know we're not soul mates, exactly, Rufus, but we've been acquainted a long time—'

'Which means you're about to say something likely to offend,' he said drily.

'I thought my mere presence in the same room was enough to do that,' she retorted, stung. 'You certainly behaved like it in the old days when—'

'When Claire was alive,' he said morosely, then gave her a long, dissecting look. 'You were rarely in my company at all, Jo. You took good care not to be.'

'It seemed the best way to make life easy for Claire,' said Jo quietly.

'Life usually was easy for Claire.' Rufus leaned forward, his hands clasped between his knees. 'It was a damnable twist of fate to deny her the one re-maining thing she lacked—and wanted more than anything else in the world.'

'A child.'

He nodded, a bitter twist to his mouth. 'Odd, really. Two normal, healthy people get married and a child is the usual outcome. But not in our case. And the worst part was that Claire began to feel she'd failed me. I won't deny I wanted a child. I did. I still do, very much. But no matter how much I told Claire I loved her, child or no child, that we could adopt if necessary, it was no use.'

Rufus ran an unsteady hand through his damp hair. 'Poor darling, she became obsessed—swallowed handfuls of vitamins, checked her temperature constantly so she'd know when she was most fertile, could hardly talk of anything else. She insisted we made love only when the time was right—' He shot a sudden, appalled look at Jo. 'Forgive me. You don't want to hear this.'

'I knew some of it,' she muttered, staring down at her clasped hands. 'Not anything private, of course, but I knew about the ever present thermometer and the vitamin-E pills, the special diet. I looked on it all as another good reason for staying single.'

Rufus frowned, his eyes questioning. 'But you *were* going to marry someone, Jo. I've only just discovered you called it off.'

'Yes. It didn't work out.' She shrugged. 'I like men. They like me. But these days I enjoy coming home here and closing the door on the world.' She gave him a wry little smile. 'I was brought up in a household with a strong female majority. I adored my father, but other than him, a man has never been vitally necessary to my life.'

'What about sex?' said Rufus baldly.

'Well, yes. A man's necessary then, of course.' Jo looked away, colouring. 'But, since you've brought the subject up, I admit I can live quite happily without a sexual relationship.'

'You're fortunate.'

'Ah, but you're a man.'

Rufus' dark, narrowed eyes met hers. 'You never seemed aware of the fact.'

'Of course I was,' she said impatiently. 'You're not the sort of man to go unnoticed. But you were— well . . .'

'Someone you disliked.'

'No,' she said, with more truth than he knew. 'Just not my style, I suppose.'

'You're very polite. Do you still feel the same about me, Jo?' he asked, surprising her.

If she'd conned herself into thinking she didn't, one look at him tonight had demonstrated beyond all doubt that she did. 'I haven't thought about you in a long time,' she said, crossing mental fingers at the lie.

'I think it was always your damnable honesty I couldn't cope with,' he said bitterly. 'It does damn all for a man's ego to know he's not worth a woman's consideration.'

'I should imagine, Rufus Grierson, that you've had plenty of consideration from a great many women over the past year—an eligible widower in need of consolation,' she added deliberately.

'The operative word, Jo Fielding, is widower,' he pointed out with stark emphasis. 'A grieving widower, I might remind you.'

His reminder was hardly necessary, thought Jo miserably. After Claire he probably couldn't bear the thought of any other woman. 'But you must have been invited to a good many dinner parties in the past few months.'

'Invited, yes. But unless the dinners were legal, all-male affairs I've rarely accepted.'

'Why not?'

'Apart from the obvious, old-fashioned reason of being in mourning for my wife, I prefer to avoid being paired with anyone, even at a dinner table,' Rufus said bluntly. 'I'm a normal sort of male. Among the things I miss from my marriage the sex is by no means the least. But I won't buy it. Nor will I mislead any woman who's convinced I'm contemplating marriage again.'

Jo digested this in silence. 'But surely you will marry again, one day?' she asked eventually.

'Who knows?' Rufus looked at his watch. 'It's late. I should go. But I dislike the thought of leaving you alone here in the dark.'

'I'll be fine,' Jo assured him, though in her heart of hearts she wasn't relishing a night alone in the big old house without a light. But she wanted Rufus to stay longer for more reasons than a mere fear of the dark.

'I'd prefer to wait for a while,' said Rufus abruptly.

'Then by all means do.' She smiled a little. 'One of the advantages of my particular lifestyle is not having to get up at the crack of dawn if I don't want to.'

Rufus subjected her to a long, dissecting scrutiny. 'You've changed a lot in a year, Jo. You look older.'

'Gee, thanks! Maturity setting in,' she said flippantly.

'I put it badly. You always looked years younger than Claire, though I knew you weren't.'

'A year younger, to be precise. We're both September birthdays, but she was the oldest in the class and I was the youngest.'

'And the cleverest, too, according to Claire. I was given chapter and verse about your exam results.'

'No wonder you took a dislike to me!' Jo pulled a face. 'I don't know about the cleverest, but I was certainly the cheekiest. At home everyone was encouraged to have their say, even the youngest like me. At school this was a disadvantage. I was always being told to stop talking, behave myself, sit up straight, and so on. Claire was so different in every way—pretty as a picture, popular with staff and classmates, and as good as gold, always.'

'Always,' he agreed, then smiled crookedly. 'You know, it's good to have her name crop up naturally; I'm grateful for your forbearance, Jo. A late-night visitor must be the last thing you need after your stint at the Mitre. I caught sight of you there and acted on impulse.'

'Impulse isn't something I associate with you, Rufus.'

'No,' he agreed. 'Not my style. Not that you have the least idea of what I'm really like.'

'You always disapproved of me—admit it!'

Rufus shook his head, frowning. 'I didn't, you know. Though I admit I couldn't see why you and Claire were so close. Two more contrasting types would be hard to find.'

'True. But somehow we just gelled from the moment we met, that first day in school. Where appearance was concerned, it was a different story. When we were in uniform it wasn't so bad, but out of school hours the contrast was painful.'

'Clothes don't interest you?' he asked curiously.

Jo shook her head at him. 'Of course they do. I'm a normal female, Rufus!'

'You always wore jeans a lot. I hardly recognised you tonight.'

'If that's a compliment, thank you,' she said tartly, then glanced down disparagingly. 'This is the type of gear I stick to for my job at the Mitre. Tailored shirt, respectable dark skirt, discreet make-up, hair braided back.'

'Otherwise the punters get familiar?' he queried drily.

She nodded. 'It's been known.'

'But do you keep all men at arm's length, Jo?'

'No, not at all. I have several men *friends*,' she said with emphasis. 'Not lovers, boyfriends or prospective husbands. Just friends.'

'If you were any other woman I wouldn't believe you,' said Rufus in a considering tone, as though he were weighing up some legal problem. 'Personally, I've never been a believer in truly platonic relationships between the sexes.'

'No,' she said coolly. 'A man like you wouldn't. Nevertheless, it's perfectly possible, I assure you.'

'From your point of view, perhaps. I doubt if the men in question agree.'

'Whether they do or not they keep their opinions to themselves,' she said flatly. 'I've no intention of falling in love. Ever. I'm just not the type to get wrapped up in a man the way Claire was in you. You were the centre of her universe. Her life revolved around you. I can't imagine feeling like that about any man. The only other male she was ever interested in was her horse—' Jo went cold, cursing her unruly tongue. 'Oh, Lord, I'm so *sorry*, Rufus.'

'Don't be. It's the truth.'

Jo sighed. 'Well, as we're on the subject, I could never understand how her horse came to throw her. Claire was such a good horsewoman.'

'She must have lost her concentration,' said Rufus, the lines deepening from nose to mouth. 'She was in a state that morning because nature had just informed her she wasn't pregnant. Every month it was the same, and there was nothing I could do to comfort her. To "blow the blues away", as she put it, she'd go off on that damned horse and gallop up on the heath until she felt better.'

'Yet she wasn't on the heath when it happened,' said Jo sadly.

'No.' His eyes darkened. 'She was just hacking along a bridle-path she'd used for years. Something spooked the horse—a squirrel probably, or a rabbit. Claire was thrown, the strap of her hat snapped and her head struck an outcropping of rock. Death,' said Rufus, his voice cracking, 'was instantaneous.' He shuddered. 'I was told to be grateful for that.'

'Don't.' Impulsively, Jo jumped from her chair and went to sit beside him, putting her hand on his. Rufus took it, holding it so tightly that she thought the bones would crack.

'I shouldn't have said that.' He frowned as he saw the glimmer of tears on her cheeks in the candlelight. 'Hell, I've made you cry. Jo, I'm sorry. Come here.' He drew her into his arms and held her close, her face against his shoulder.

'Do you know, I've never cried for Claire before?' she said, her tear-thickened voice muffled against his jacket. 'I longed to. But I never could.'

'Then it's time you did,' he said huskily, and smoothed a hand over her hair. The light, delicate touch snapped her self-control. Jo sagged against him, racked by sobs, and Rufus Grierson held her tightly, his own body taut with answering emotion as he waited for the storm to pass.

'I'm ruining your jacket,' Jo said hoarsely at last, and Rufus sat her upright and stripped the jacket off, before returning her to her place against his shoulder.

'Soak the shirt as much as you like,' he said gruffly, and Jo gave a strangled little sound, half-laugh, half-hiccup.

Rufus held her closer and patted her back, his hand warm through the thin cotton of her shirt. Eventually the hand stilled and lay heavy between her shoulderblades and Jo tensed and tried to sit up, but the hand was like iron on her back, holding her solidly against his chest.

Jo raised her face in entreaty. 'Rufus—' She stopped, her heart thudding as her eyes met a look of such blind need that she trembled violently. Then his mouth was on hers, and she gasped and tried to push him away, but he held her fast, his mouth softening, coaxing, his tongue persistent. Her disobedient lips parted and, undermined by the rarity of her tears, Jo's resistance was nil when his arms tightened round her.

The heat from his body ignited her response in a way he recognised and reacted to, nurturing the flame with caresses which took her breath away. A shudder ran through him, and his hands and mouth moved over her with such sure, importuning skill that she was defenceless, not only before the driving force of his need, but before her own, incontrollable response to it.

She was where she'd always longed to be, and she shook from head to foot, vulnerable to his urgent, itinerant mouth and skilled, disrobing hands, with neither will nor desire to prevent the urgent male body when, at last, it sought the release denied it during the past lonely months. As they came together all the grief and pent-up emotions of the past year engulfed them, welding them together in a desperate need for consolation which quickly transformed into unimagined, overwhelming rapture and brought them rapidly to shared, gasping culmination.

Then the overhead light came on.

Jo wrenched herself free and dived for her clothes, her averted face scarlet with embarrassment as she fled, heart pounding, to the sanctuary of the bathroom. What, in heaven's name, had *possessed* her? She looked at herself in the mirror and shuddered, pulling on her clothes at top speed. Given the choice, she thought savagely, she would stay in the bathroom indefinitely, until Rufus took the hint and went away. But his manners were too good to allow him to do that, of course.

It was a good ten minutes before she felt sufficiently recovered to emerge from the bathroom, fully dressed, face repaired, tangled hair brushed free of its unravelling braid, to confront Rufus Grierson.

Instead of sitting on the sofa, superior and unmoved, without a hair out of place, as she'd expected, Rufus was in the kitchen, filling her kettle.

'You said you were yearning for tea,' he said calmly.

But Jo wasn't listening. Now Rufus' thick coppery hair had dried out a gleaming layer of silver lay over the surface, like a coating of frost on autumn leaves. The contrast with his bronzed face and dark eyes was dramatic.

He smiled a little. 'I didn't turn white with shock while you were in the bathroom. The process started when Claire died.'

Claire. A burning tide of colour swept up Jo's throat and face, then receded again below the blue and white stripes of her shirt, leaving her face sallow and colourless beneath a tan darker than Rufus Grierson's.

He switched the kettle on, then leaned against the kitchen counter, arms folded as he watched her colour recede. 'You are now racked with guilt and about to hurl recriminations at my head.'

Jo squared her shoulders. 'No. We're both adults, Rufus. We know that what happened was—was just a mutual need for comfort. You say you haven't slept with a woman since Claire died; tonight you were missing her more than usual, and when I cried you comforted me. I quite understand.' Which was true enough. She understood only too well. Her role in the proceedings had been as substitute for Rufus Grierson's beautiful, dead Claire.

Rufus went on gazing at her with the same, disquieting look.

Jo motioned him out of the way as the kettle boiled. She put teabags in a pot, poured in boiling water, put the lid on, then turned to look at him. 'Look, Rufus,' she said rather desperately, 'let's not beat about the bush. What happened tonight was the natural outcome of shared grief. The fact that we've never been—well, close before was irrelevant at that particular moment in time. It was your anniversary and you badly needed—'

'I didn't come here looking for sex,' he said with sudden, fierce distaste. 'It never entered my head. I just came to hand over the earrings and maybe talk for a while. As I did until you cried.' He frowned. 'Claire told me often that you never cried over anything, even as a little girl.'

'True. But I'm only human,' said Jo forlornly.

'So am I, Jo Fielding, so am I!' Rufus caught her hand in his. 'Are you waiting for an apology for what happened just now? I'd be lying if I said I was sorry.' His eyes held hers intently. 'Deprivation obviously had something to do with it on my part, as did our emotions for both of us. Nevertheless, what we shared together was no run-of-the-mill sexual experience. For me, anyway.'

'For me too,' said Jo, incurably honest. Her eyes fell. 'Which doesn't make it any easier. I feel so *guilty*.'

'So do I.' He breathed in deeply. 'Even though I'm utterly certain Claire would understand.'

'Probably she would,' said Jo wretchedly. 'She always had a much nicer nature than mine. Though she might have understood more easily if it was someone else. Not me.'

Rufus made no attempt to deny it, and an awkward silence fell between them.

'I'd better go,' he said at last.

'Would you like some tea first?' she felt obliged to ask.

He shook his head. 'No, thanks. Goodnight, Jo.'

'Goodnight.' She walked with him to the door, feeling as gauche and awkward as a schoolgirl. 'Thank you for bringing the earrings. I'll take great care of them.'

Rufus reached a hand inside his jacket and took out his wallet. He took a card from it and gave it to her. 'This is my new address and telephone number. If you need me call me.'

Jo took the card without argument, but with no intention of ringing Rufus Grierson, ever. 'Goodbye, Rufus. The landing lights are automatic. They'll switch off once you've closed the outer door downstairs.'

He looked down into her eyes for a moment. 'Are you sure you're all right, Jo?'

She met the look squarely. 'Yes. I'm fine.'

To her surprise he took her by the shoulders and kissed her cheek. 'Goodnight, Jo. Take care.'

'You too,' she said huskily, and watched him as he went downstairs and out of sight. She waited until he'd reached the floor below, then locked her door, made sure all the candles were properly snuffed, picked up a cushion which had landed on the floor at some stage. She eyed it malevolently, then perched on a kitchen stool to drink the tea she'd made and sat staring into space, depressed and shaken, feeling as though life would never be the same again. At last she heaved a sigh and trudged off to have a bath, then groaned in frustration at the sight of Rufus Grierson's expensive raincoat hanging in the shower stall.

Jo hurried through her bath, pulled on a T-shirt and dived into bed, determined to erase the events of the past few hours from her mind. There was no point in dwelling on it, telling herself she should have protested louder, fought harder—done *something*. Because she hadn't. Quite simply, it had been impossible to resist the man she'd fallen in love with the first time she'd ever set eyes on him. She could only hope that after tonight he still had no idea how she felt.

While Claire was alive she'd worked hard to preserve the fiction that Jo Fielding and Rufus Grierson would never be friends. On Rufus' part, of course, this had been true enough. He probably hadn't given her a thought all this past year while he was grieving for Claire. Jo shivered. The last thing Rufus Grierson had intended was making love to her tonight, she knew perfectly well. He had come to deliver the earrings and just talk about his dead wife with someone who—in an entirely different way—had loved Claire as much as he did.

For a woman who cried once in a blue moon, Jo told herself bitterly, tonight, of all nights, had not been a good time to emote all over Rufus Grierson. Not that she'd chosen to cry. It had just happened. But if she hadn't cried Rufus wouldn't have taken her in his arms to comfort her, and she wouldn't have lost control—and neither would he. She groaned aloud and turned out the light, needing the dark.

Sleep was hard to come by. To her fury the moment Jo closed her eyes she kept reliving the entire disturbing episode from beginning to end, and at last lay staring, wide-eyed, into the darkness, searching for something to occupy her mind, to blot out the sheer magic of a pleasure she'd never experienced before.

In college there'd been Linus Cole, the postgraduate student who'd dazzled the little freshman with his attentions, and introduced her to what he'd referred to with relish as 'the pleasures of the flesh'. Then, instead of producing a ring as she'd naïvely expected, he went off to take up his fellowship at Cambridge without a backward glance. Thereafter Jo had firmly kept the rest of marauding student manhood at arm's length. It was much later on in her career that she met Edward Hyde, and for a while had even become engaged to him.

Jo sighed. She'd been madly in love with Linus, and very fond of Edward, but neither of them had come remotely near giving her the pleasure experienced tonight with Rufus. She ground her teeth, tossed and turned, got up and made herself some tea, went back to bed, and still couldn't sleep. And in her efforts to blot out Rufus' lovemaking she let herself think instead of the last time they'd met—a harrowing occasion she normally tried not to think of at all.

CHAPTER TWO

IT HAD been a hot August day of bright sunlight and clear blue skies: weather more suitable for a wedding than a funeral.

For the first time in their acquaintance, the two people facing each other across the open grave had something in common. They were the only dry-eyed mourners as the clergyman read the service of committal. Jo stood, rigid, enduring, dazed by the utter unreality of the situation. On such a glorious day it was so hard to believe that Claire—beautiful, warm, loving Claire—had gone for ever. The scent of recently scythed grass lay heavy in the air, bringing back memories of long summer holidays when both schoolgirls had savoured every moment before the autumn term put an end to summer idleness.

Contributions to charity had been requested instead of flowers, but a single floral tribute lay on the gleaming oak lid of the coffin. Jo stared numbly at the replica of the wedding bouquet that Claire had carried two years earlier when she'd married the man who stood, still as a statue, on the opposite side of the grave. Jo kept her eyes averted from his grief. She looked down steadfastly on the madonna lilies and yellow rosebuds, and shivered as the first handful of earth hit the coffin.

At last it was over. Jo waited her turn among the mourners, then held out a hand to Rufus Grierson and murmured a conventional word of condolence. He took the hand for a moment in a hard grasp, said something appropriate in clipped, disciplined tones. Jo moved on to exchange embraces with Claire's devastated parents, and, much against her will, promised to go back to the imposing Victorian house where Claire had grown up. Refusing a lift, she set off alone.

Hot in the navy linen dress borrowed from her sister, Jo walked slowly, sure she would cry at last once she was alone. But the relief of tears never came. She had dreaded the ritual of muted voices over canapés and sherry, but knew it would give some small measure of comfort to Claire's parents. For the past week they had been caught up, like Rufus, in the organisation of funeral arrangements. But Jo was sure their loss would finally strike home when all was quiet and the last guest had gone. It would be the same for Rufus, of course, but he could one day find himself another wife. The Beaumonts could never replace their only child. There wasn't even a grandchild to give them solace, despite Claire's desperate desire to get pregnant.

'I'm not even thirty yet, Jo,' she'd said, just a few short weeks earlier. 'There's all sorts of treatment I still haven't tried. I've got loads of time.'

But Claire had run out of time one fine summer morning.

Jo came to with a start as a car glided to a halt just ahead of her. 'I'll give you a lift,' said Rufus, leaning over to open the passenger door for her.

The last thing Jo's battered emotions needed was a ride in a car alone with Rufus. She got in reluctantly, and fastened the seat belt. 'I thought you were with the others,' she said, her heart contracting at the bleak, weary look on his face.

'I needed to be on my own for a while.'

'Yes,' agreed Jo sombrely. 'I was walking for the same reason.' She turned to him hastily. 'Though I appreciate the lift, of course.'

'No need to be polite, Jo,' he snapped, then touched a hand fleetingly to hers in apology. 'Sorry. I'm on edge.'

As well he might be, thought Jo with compassion, glad when the car turned down the narrow lane towards the Beaumonts' house. Rufus parked the car at the end of a long line of others and Jo got out to walk beside him along the familiar driveway to the open front door.

'God, I wish this were over,' said Rufus, with sudden, quiet violence.

'So do I.' Jo's teeth sank into her quivering bottom lip.

He looked down into her face, and breathed out slowly. 'Of course you do.' To her surprise he took her hand and held it tightly for a moment. 'All right?'

She nodded mutely, and his face relaxed a little.

'Come on, then. Let's face the music.'

The Beaumonts were in the hall, in unconscious parody of a receiving line at a wedding. They were more composed, Gloria Beaumont's eyes still red, but dry now under the stylish black hat. Ted Beaumont, large and bluff as a rule, but oddly diminished today, wrung Rufus's hand in silence, and Jo hugged Claire's mother close in wordless sympathy, then offered to help the maid with the food.

'Oh, my dear, would you?' said Gloria in gratitude.

'I'll see to the drinks,' said Rufus.

Keeping herself occupied helped Jo to deal with the situation. And, she suspected, it was the same for Rufus. Elegant as always in sombre bespoke tailoring, he circulated with glasses and decanters, evading long exchanges with any group other than his family. Jo served guests with delicious titbits and stifled a searing dart of pain when she found they came from the bakery who'd once provided cream cakes for two hungry schoolgirls. As she moved through the room Jo's fragile composure was tested to the utmost by condolences from people who knew how close she'd been to Claire.

At last Ted Beaumont closed the door on the final, sombre face with a sigh of relief, and urged Jo to stay to dinner.

'Sorry, I can't,' said Jo, desperate to get away. 'I'm working tonight.'

'Couldn't they give you the night off in the circumstances?' pleaded Gloria Beaumont.

Jo shook her head, feeling guilty. 'Two of the others are on holiday. I can't really let them down. I should have been working at lunchtime today as it was.'

Rufus frowned. 'I thought you worked in the evenings.'

'As I said—it's holiday time. I've been filling in.' Jo smiled apologetically. 'The extra money comes in useful.'

'At least let Rufus drive you home,' said Ted. 'I would myself, but I've had a drop too much to drink.'

Jo shook her head. 'No, really. I need some fresh air before my stint at the Mitre.' And, more than fresh air, she needed time to herself to say her last, private goodbyes to Claire.

Rufus saw her out and accompanied her down to the gates, his eyes bloodshot and his face colourless, despite the heat.

'Are you sure about walking?' he asked. 'Let me run you home.'

'It's very kind of you, but I'd rather walk. I *need* to walk,' she added unsteadily.

The evening sun outlined Rufus' hair with fire as he looked down at her. 'You look exhausted. And you've lost weight.'

'It's the dress. It's a size too big—and I look terrible in navy. I borrowed it from my sister. None of my things were suitable for the—the occasion.' Abruptly Jo came to the end of her tether. 'Goodbye, Rufus. I really must go.'

'I'll ring you,' he said.

'That's probably not a good idea—'

'As you wish,' he said instantly.

She watched, dismayed, as every vestige of warmth vanished from his face. She had meant it wasn't a good idea for the time being. Not for ever. But something in Rufus' manner made it impossible to explain.

He inclined his head formally. 'I'll say goodbye, Jo.'

She gave him a depressed little nod, hesitated, then turned and walked away, utterly dejected.

It was better this way, she told herself firmly. A clean break with Rufus was best all round. She must forget him. Even with Claire dead Jo knew she had no hope of succeeding her friend in Rufus' affections. Claire had been beautiful both by nature and to look at, her only aim in life to please the husband who was so much her intellectual superior. Jo knew she could never be like that. She was neither as beautiful as Claire nor as compliant. She would find it impossible to live her life merely as an extension of some man— even a man like Rufus Grierson. Yet, to be fair, Claire had been ideally happy with her marriage, apart from her inability to give Rufus a child.

Weariness put an end to Jo's introspection. The early-evening sunshine was hot as she trudged down the road, and the headache she'd been holding at bay homed in as she let go the iron control she'd exerted all afternoon. But still the tears refused to flow—for Claire, or for Rufus.

It would have done her good to cry that day, she thought now, in the sleepless dark of the present. It might have eased her aching sense of loss.

At the age of ten Jo Fielding had won a scholarship to the expensive school where she met Claire Beaumont on the first day and began a friendship which ended only with Claire's death. The bond between two such very different children was a mystery to everyone who knew them. Claire had needed special, expensive tuition to help her pass the entrance examination to the highly academic school, while Jo, almost a year younger, had done so well that her scholarship paid the fees for her entire school career. Claire was tall for her age, well behaved, blonde and rounded, her school uniform always immaculate, Jo inches shorter, wiry, brown-skinned, black-haired and mischievous and rarely tidy from the moment she left home.

Eventually Claire went to a finishing school in Switzerland and Jo to university to read English, but their relationship survived surprisingly well. Inevitably they saw less of each other, but when they were both in Pennington they picked up where they'd left off and spent as much time as they could together, swapping boasts about boyfriends and roaring with laughter over anecdotes from their vastly disparate lives.

Claire learned cordon bleu cooking, the art of entertaining, and how to make the most of her already dazzling looks. Her flawless skin and blue eyes were framed by corn-coloured hair cut by a master hand, and she wore simple, understated clothes with world-famous labels.

Jo shared a chaotic household with several students of both sexes and ate junk food, all her spare cash spent on books. Her wiry, boyish figure soon became skinny, and her dark hair, worn long to save expense, lost its gloss. She studied hard, enjoyed tutorials, and sat for hours with her peers in the students' union over half a pint of lager, arguing hotly about putting the world to rights. To her mother's despair she dressed in leggings teamed with sweaters from charity shops and cadged cast-offs from her sisters for her bar job at the Mitre during vacations.

The twins, who by this time both had high-powered jobs in banking, despaired of turning their ugly duckling of a sister into a swan, then one day realised they didn't have to. Jo achieved a very good degree, followed it with a course in computers, then got a job with the *Pennington Gazette*. From then on she paid more attention to clothes, rounded out on her mother's cooking, and, though never as opulently curved as Claire, at least looked like the female she was, rather than her sisters' skinny little brother.

And all the time her friendship with Claire never wavered, not even when Rufus Grierson came on the scene. Jo, who had already been a bridesmaid at her sisters' double wedding, hadn't the heart to refuse Claire the same service, and followed the radiant bride down the aisle, wearing an amber chiffon dress which cost more than all her other clothes put together. Then she'd come face to face with Rufus for the first time during all the kissing and uproar in the vestry, and felt as if she'd been struck by lightning. Having never fallen in love before—not really, she realised—she wasn't prepared for the shock of it, and afterwards remembered very little of Claire's wedding day, other than her certainty that Claire's marriage marked the end of their friendship.

Jo was proved wrong. Rufus soon learned that the time she spent with Jo was important to his wife, and if he had any objections, which Jo was sure he had, kept them to himself. And to make sure Claire never knew how she felt about Rufus Jo took care never to be around when he was at home, and accepted invitations to the Griersons' social functions only when there was a crowd of other guests. The arrangement worked surprisingly well, and, most important of all, Claire never suffered any hurt.

Jo sighed and punched her pillow for the umpteenth time. Claire's tragically early death had left such a gaping hole. Now Jo sometimes went to London to meet an old college friend, but in Pennington her social life had rather ground to a halt

since she'd embarked on her novel. She gritted her
teeth in the darkness. It was time she joined something. A gym or a badminton club, or maybe a writers'
circle. She might even accept some of the invitations
she received over the bar at the Mitre. The respectable
ones, anyway. And if Rufus Grierson ever turned up
on her doorstep again—which was highly unlikely—
next time, however much she wanted to, she wouldn't
invite him in. Not, of course, that there was the
slightest danger of a rerun of tonight's episode.

A shiver ran through her at the thought. Stop that,
she told herself savagely. The sensible thing was to
look on what happened as a learning experience.
Tonight she'd discovered that her two former experi-
ences had been no preparation at all for what happened with Rufus. And it had surprisingly little to do
with expertise. Linus had prided himself on his skill,
and Edward had been warm and loving, but with
Rufus she'd caught fire at the first touch of his mouth,
and, unless she was mistaken, it had been just the
same for him. She shivered again. For someone she'd
always thought of as totally self-contained, Rufus
Grierson had lost his cool with a vengeance. Human
after all. Yet Claire had put him on a pedestal right
from the start, and spent the rest of her all too short
life in trying to live up to him.

Jo got up next morning, eyeing her reflection and
Rufus Grierson's raincoat with equal dislike. The day
was bright and sunny, and a lot fresher than the sultry
heat of the past few days, but Jo's mood was dark.
She pulled on denim shorts and a halter top, went
downstairs to collect her daily paper, and had just

settled down with a cup of tea to read it when her phone rang.

'Jo?'

Her heart gave a sickening thump in her chest, and it took one or two deep, calming breaths before she could answer. 'Hello, Rufus. You left your raincoat here.'

'Did I?'

'Isn't that why you're ringing?'

'No, it's not.'

'Oh.'

'How are you this morning?'

Jo thrust a shaky hand through her hair. 'Tired. I didn't sleep much.'

'It may sound insensitive, but *I* slept like a log.' He paused. 'I want to see you. We should talk.'

'*No!* I mean—I'd rather not, Rufus. I'll take your raincoat to the Mitre tonight. You can pick it up there—preferably during the day when I'm not around.'

The ensuing silence was so long that Jo was about to hang up when Rufus spoke again.

'I don't blame you for your attitude,' he said, sounding so detached and impersonal that Jo scowled. 'My behaviour was inexcusable.'

'Not really,' she responded slowly, trying to be fair. 'We were both off balance, emotionally. And I was equally to blame. I should have put up more resistance.'

'It wouldn't have made any difference,' he assured her. 'For the first time in my life I lost control, and there was nothing a pint-sized adversary like you could have done, believe me.'

'Nevertheless I'd feel a lot happier this morning if I'd done *something*,' said Jo bitterly.

'Would you be angry if I said you did something very important from my point of view?'

'It depends on what it was.'

'You gave me the best night's sleep I've had in months. You needed comfort, I provided it—then we both succumbed to the most potent form of it the male and female of the species can give each other.'

'How clinical!'

He laughed, sounding very unlike the Rufus Grierson she thought she knew. 'Clinical's the last word to describe what happened between us last night, Jo.'

'Please—I don't want to discuss it any more,' she said, flustered. 'Thank you for ringing. I'll make sure you get your raincoat. Goodbye.' And before Rufus could say another word she put the receiver back and leaned against the wall, shaken and breathless.

Deciding her blood sugars were low, Jo made herself some coffee and toast, piled the latter with her mother's marmalade and read the *Gazette* diligently while she ate. For once, she decided afterwards, she would take a day off from her word processor. There was an end-of-term feeling about the weather. She would go up to the flat roof over her kitchen and soak up what might very well be the last really hot sunshine of the summer.

Jo's glowing tan had been acquired over several weeks of unusually consistent hot weather on her private bit of roof, which covered the kitchen and bathroom extension built onto the attic flat. She collected sunglasses, straw hat, book, a couple of cushions, a bottle of sun oil, and climbed out over her window-boxes to her private little eyrie. She rubbed herself with oil, let herself down on the cushions, tilted the hat over her eyes and decided she wouldn't read until later.

It was the last thought she had for some time. Jo woke with a start to find that the sun had moved a long way from its original position and she'd been asleep for the best part of three hours. Thirsty and hot, Jo passed her belongings through the window, wriggled through after them, drank down two glasses of water, then went off to read the neglected book in the bath.

The Mitre was an eighteenth-century coaching inn between Gloucester and Pennington, and had been enlarged and renovated with taste to house three bars and a separate restaurant. For the time being, while two of the staff were on holiday Jo, Phil Dexter the manager, and Tim, the young man working his way through his hotel management course, manned the bars between them in the evenings, while Phil's wife, Louise, ran the restaurant with an efficient pair of waitresses.

When Jo reported for work that evening Phil Dexter eyed her with appreciation.

'What a tan! Up on the roof again?'

'Too long this time,' she said ruefully. 'I fell asleep.'

'You look stunning,' he assured her. 'Good for trade.'

Jo usually wore something a little more festive on Saturday evenings. Her jade-green shirt looked good with the glow of her tan, and instead of weaving her newly washed hair into a French plait she'd tied it back with a green ribbon at the nape of her neck. With eyes emphasised more than usual and her favourite silver hoops in her ears, Jo felt she'd done her best.

Louise Dexter smiled as she passed on her way through the restaurant. 'You look good, Jo. Something nice happened today?'

'Not really. It must be the tan.'

'If you say so. I thought a new man, maybe.'

'No fear. Married to my computer, that's me!'

They laughed together, then Jo turned her smile on her first customer. 'Good evening. What can I get you?'

A few minutes later the usual Saturday rush was in full swing.

'Phew!' muttered Jo at one stage. 'I'm glad I'm not in tomorrow.'

'Lucky old you,' said Tim enviously. 'Can you hold the fort a minute? Time I collected glasses.'

'Right.' Jo turned back to the bar to find Rufus leaning against it.

'Good evening, Jo,' he said affably. 'Scotch and soda, please.'

Jo fought her heart back from her throat to its normal location and complied without a word, hoping her tan hid the flaring colour in her face. To have Rufus materialise on the other side of the bar threw her into a confusion she hadn't felt since she was eighteen and pursued by the worldly Linus.

She took the proffered banknote and gave him the requisite change, glad she had an electronic till to do the sums. 'Two evenings on the run at the Mitre, Rufus?'

'There's no law against it, Jo.'

'No, but a touch different from your usual social round, surely?'

'You know nothing about my social life,' he said without rancour.

'True. But I've never seen you here before,' she pointed out. 'I thought the Chesterton would be more your kind of thing.'

'I use it to entertain clients, I grant you, but the man I brought here yesterday was very impressed with the meal. Until last night I had no idea you still worked here,' he added, and smiled. 'I'll come here more often in the future.'

Jo turned away to serve another customer, and by the time she was free again Rufus was sitting at a table, talking to a vivacious blonde with a tan almost as dark as her own. After the long, hot summer tanned faces were common, but the blonde was pretty, and very animated as she laughed with Rufus, who looked suitably attentive. As he was more than entitled to do, Jo reminded herself, furious to discover she felt jealous. But she had always known that Rufus was unlikely to remain a widower for ever, nor would generous Claire have wanted him to.

Depressed by the superiority of Claire's nature to her own, Jo was glad to be kept busy by the usual organised chaos of Saturday evening, and had no more opportunity for speculation on the social life of Rufus Grierson until closing time. When Phil rang the bell for 'time' Jo sighed with relief, and craned her neck to see across the still crowded room, but there was no sign of Rufus and his attractive blonde companion. They were probably on the way back to Rufus' new home right this minute, thought Jo bitterly. He had obviously decided his year of mourning was up.

Jo collected her bicycle from one of the Mitre storerooms, wheeled it across the rapidly emptying car park, and found Rufus Grierson leaning against a car under the light near the exit.

'I'll stow that in the back of the car and drive you home,' he informed her, and grasped the handlebars.

Jo, torn between delight at the sight of him and anger at his pre-emptive manner, scowled irritably. 'No, thanks. I *like* to ride home.'

'After the night you've just spent in there?' he said, shaking his head. 'Come off it, Jo. You looked fit to drop by closing time.'

'I thought you'd gone, long before then,' she said coldly.

'We moved into the other bar when Rory arrived.' He looked down into her blank face. 'My brother, Rory, in case you've forgotten. And Susannah, his bride-to-be.'

So the blonde belonged to his brother. To her shame Jo's spirits soared.

'It's taking you a long time to accept a lift,' observed Rufus.

'Mainly because I can't think why you're offering it.'

'My motives are pure, I assure you,' he said sardonically. 'You're tired; I'm here with a car.'

'But *why* are you here?'

'It seemed the best way to achieve conversation with you, Jo Fielding.' He frowned. 'I was worried about you.'

'Worried? About *me*?' Her eyes widened incredulously.

'Look,' he said impatiently. 'Couldn't we continue this in the car? The bike comes apart, I assume?'

'No need; I'll leave it here. I do sometimes, if I get a lift.'

'So I'm allowed to drive you home?'

'Yes.' Jo looked him in the eye. 'But only as far as the front gate.'

'Don't worry. All I ask is a few minutes' conversation, not a repeat of last night—ravishing experience though it was,' he added deliberately.

Jo wrenched the handlebars away from him and wheeled the bike back across the car park. When she rejoined Rufus he was standing where she'd left him, swinging car keys from a long forefinger.

'It's a different car,' commented Jo as he handed her in.

'I got rid of the other one after the funeral.'

Which put an end to conversation until they reached the quiet, tree-lined streets on the outskirts of town, when Jo broke the silence to ask what Rufus wanted to talk about.

'Is it something to do with Claire?' she asked warily.

'No.' Rufus turned into Bruton Road, where Jo lived in one of a row of tall Edwardian houses converted into flats. He killed the lights, then undid his seat belt and turned towards her purposefully. 'I'd like some information.'

She frowned. 'What information do I have that can possibly interest you, Rufus? How to pull a pint? Or is it something to do with my work? If so, no chance.

Reporters never reveal their sources—especially to devious lawyers!'

'I'm neither devious nor interested in you as a journalist—'

'I find it hard to believe you're interested in me at all,' she snapped. 'So get to the point.'

'I will if you'll be quiet long enough to let me,' he said irascibly, and drew in a deep breath. 'Let's start again. Jo, did you mean what you said last night about not having a lover?'

She gave him a startled look. Surely Rufus wasn't proposing himself for the post? She thrust the dizzying thought away, and assured him there was no man in her life at the present.

'Not even one of those platonic friends you talked about?'

'No. Since I started on my novel my social life has dwindled to nothing except for the odd party at Thalia's, or Callie's.' Jo grinned suddenly. 'My sisters insist I socialise now and then. They're convinced I'll turn odd and become a recluse.'

'Difficult to be reclusive while you work at the Mitre,' he observed. 'I was watching you tonight. You're very popular with the customers. It's a clever balancing act.'

She raised an eyebrow. 'Balancing act?'

'Friendly and warm, but also brisk and efficient.'

'Thank you. I do my best. Even so from time to time some man gets the wrong impression. But Phil— the manager—is always on the alert. He's an expert at pouring oil on troubled waters.' Jo gazed at him searchingly. 'So what else did you want to know?'

Rufus turned to meet the scrutiny. 'It's difficult to express it without giving you offence, but, to be blunt, I need to know whether you've slept with anyone else recently.'

'*What?*' Jo glared at him, incensed. 'It's absolutely none of your business who I sleep with.'

'In this instance it is,' he said with finality. 'So tell me, Jo. Before last night when was the last time you made love?'

Instead of slapping his face, Jo reached for the seat belt and undid it clumsily, so angry that her fingers were trembling. But before she could jump from the car Rufus caught her by the arm.

'Calm down. I'm not asking out of prurient curiosity.'

'I fail to see why you're asking me at all!'

'Answer me first, then I'll give you my reasons.'

Jo stared into his intent face for a moment, then shrugged indifferently. 'If you must know, I haven't had a relationship of that kind for a long time. I don't sleep around. Just before Claire died I met a man called Edward Hyde, who works for my sister's husband. After the funeral I was very down. Edward was kind and sympathetic and I was lonely, so when he asked me to marry him I said yes.' She sighed. 'It was a mistake. I discovered he wanted to change my lifestyle completely. I could have given up the bar work without a backward glance, of course, but not the writing. So that was that. If Edward hadn't been so sweet when I was grieving for Claire I wouldn't have said yes in the first place. So I gave him back his ring.'

'When?'

She shrugged irritably. 'I can't remember to the exact second! Some time in November, last year.'

'And no one since?'

'No one.' Jo eyed him militantly. 'Why do you want to know?'

'Because if you happen to get pregnant from last night I'd want to be certain I was the father,' said Rufus bluntly.

'Get lost!' she said stormily, her hand shaking with temper as she tried to get her key in the door.

Rufus took the key from her and turned it in the lock. 'It needed to be said.'

She turned on him, glaring up into his face which, to her added fury, looked as inscrutable as ever. 'Even if it did happen I wouldn't tell you, Rufus.'

'That would be very foolish,' he said, with the patience of someone talking to an unreasonable child. 'Remember what I said last night?'

'You said a lot last night,' she said tightly.

'I said I wanted a child as much as Claire did. I also said that I still do. So if you are pregnant due to my loss of control last night I will naturally take responsibility.'

Jo's eyes glittered with rage. 'Oh, you will, will you?' She gave a scornful little laugh. 'In your dreams!'

She went inside and slammed the door in his face, then ran up all the flights of stairs so fast that lights were dancing in front of her eyes by the time she was safe inside her flat. She slammed the door shut and stalked about the room like an angry tigress, vibrating with the temper she rarely lost these days. She was twenty-nine years old, she reminded herself. A grown woman shouldn't indulge in tantrums.

Nevertheless, it was a long time before Jo simmered down enough to make herself some coffee. She slumped on the sofa to drink it and worked her way through half a packet of chocolate biscuits while Rufus' words went round and round in her brain.

What if he was right? Unlike Claire she had no idea when she was fertile. And in the past contraception was something she'd firmly left to the men involved— all two of them. What an idiot! Until Rufus had brought the subject up the possibility of consequences from last night had never occurred to her. Now it would be hard to think of anything else until she knew whether she was pregnant or not.

With an anguished groan Jo went off to have a shower. And let out a screech of frustration when she found Rufus' raincoat still hanging there.

Jo got up next morning with a blinding headache, the direct result of washing down chocolate biscuits with black coffee while out of her mind with worry. As she still was, she realised bitterly, and swallowed a couple of painkillers, chewed dutifully on a plain biscuit, then moved on to several cups of tea. To add to her gloom it was raining, and because there was no delivery of newspapers on a Sunday she would have to walk to the nearest newsagent a few roads away.

Jo pulled on a raincoat and went downstairs, wincing as she came out into daylight, despite the greyness of the day. When she arrived back with her usual armful of papers the light was glowing on her answering machine. She pressed the button, then breathed in sharply as she heard Rufus' voice.

'Jo. I'm on the public phone at the Mitre. No one knows anything about my raincoat.'

Jo's headache was beginning to subside an hour later, when her doorbell rang.

'Yes?' she said, resigned, into the intercom.

'Rufus here, Jo.'

'Hello.' She sighed. 'Sorry I forgot your raincoat. You'd better come up.'

When Jo opened the door to him Rufus eyed her searchingly. 'Good morning, Jo. You look fragile.'

'Headache.' She motioned him inside. 'I'll fetch your coat.' She went to the bathroom for it, and returned to her sitting room to find Rufus sitting on her sofa reading the financial section of her paper.

'By all means make yourself at home,' she said, resorting to sarcasm to disguise her pleasure at the sight.

Rufus got up. 'Are you expecting someone?'

'No.' She breathed in deeply. 'But I feel rough. I'd very much like to be alone.'

'Do you get headaches often?'

'Only if I ignore the things that trigger them off.' She gave him a hostile look. 'I was in such a temper when I got up here last night I ate half a packet of chocolate biscuits and drank a lot of black coffee.'

The corners of his mouth twitched. 'Your cure for stress?'

'Yes. I don't smoke—and I'm never, ever drinking brandy again,' she added bitterly, eyes kindling.

'I just want a quick word, then I'll leave you in peace.'

'Right.' Jo folded her arms militantly. 'Say your word.'

'I looked at your calendar while you were in the bathroom. I gather that by next weekend you'll know whether you're pregnant or not,' he said rapidly, dumbfounding her.

Jo stared at him, outraged. 'How do you know that?' she demanded.

'You forget,' said Rufus, unmoved. 'For my poor, darling Claire life revolved latterly around certain red asterisks on the calendar. You mark yours in the same way.'

Jo's face flushed scarlet with angry embarrassment. 'This is preposterous. You've no right to trespass on my private life—'

'I agree, in every other aspect of it,' said Rufus, taking the wind out of her sails. 'In this instance I have every right.'

'It doesn't apply,' she said tightly.

'It might.' Dark eyes locked with hers. 'Claire once told me you preferred to leave contraception to the men in your life.'

Jo ground her teeth, wondering what else had Claire told him. 'Only two men ever featured in my life in that way, so it's never been a problem.' She turned away to stare out of the window across the rooftops. 'But if it's third time unlucky and I'm pregnant due to your attentions I prefer to deal with it myself.'

'What do you mean by "deal"?' he asked sharply.

She turned back to face him, head high. 'Coping. On my own. I don't need a man in my life for anything, not even as a father for this mythical child we don't even know exists yet.' She bit her lip. 'This is ridiculous, Rufus. We're both making a fuss over something that hasn't even happened yet—and probably never will.'

'I want your promise that you'll tell me if it does,' he ordered. 'I'm not leaving here until I get it.'

The look in his eyes made Jo decide that he meant what he said. 'Oh, very well,' she said wearily at last. 'I promise. Though if I say all's well how will you know if I'm lying?' she added curiously.

'Because the one thing I do know about you, Jo Fielding, is your honesty. Claire said you never lied about anything, not even to get yourself out of trouble in school,' he said, disarming her. He put his hand under her chin and raised her face. 'I'll give you some advice for free. If you take to lying regularly you'll have to control a certain little mannerism that gives you away.'

She dodged away, horrified by her body's reaction to his touch. 'What do I do? Tell me!'

'Not on your life.' Rufus laughed, his eyes dancing in a way she'd never seen before. 'I'll keep that bit of information to myself. It may come in very useful in the future.'

Jo hid her inner turmoil with a stiff little smile. 'Since we're unlikely to come into contact in the future I don't see how.'

'Who knows what the future has in store?' he returned affably. 'I'll leave you in peace to get rid of your headache.'

'Very good of you,' she said acidly, and opened the door. 'Goodbye, Rufus.'

He picked up the raincoat and went outside to the landing. 'No doubt it's pointless to ask you to ring me.'

'Utterly pointless.'

'Would it also be pointless to ask you to have dinner with me one night?'

'Yes, it would.'

'Why exactly?' he asked with interest.

'Rufus,' said Jo, wanting him to contradict her, 'you don't even like me.'

He gazed at her consideringly for a moment. 'Don't I?' he said at last, and went sauntering downstairs without waiting for a reply.

CHAPTER THREE

Jo's novel had been simmering in her brain for years before she'd finally decided that to write it she had to give up her job on Features at the *Gazette* and freelance. It was a decision she'd never had cause to regret. She'd worked up a list of profitable contacts and managed to make a very respectable living. Unknown to most people other than her family, she kept on her part-time work at the Mitre more for research for her novel than any real need to earn money.

When Rose Fielding had been persuaded to move she helped Jo find a flat, donated some furniture from the family home to furnish it, and made Jo's curtains herself before going to Oxfordshire to take up residence in the lodge Jo always referred to as the Willow Cabin, due to its location at Thalia's gate. And, faintly guilty at her pleasure in living alone, Jo had occupied her flat for six months by the time Rufus Grierson made his unexpected re-entry into her life.

'You'll be lonely and get all reclusive and peculiar, living alone and not seeing anybody,' had been her sisters' comment. Rose Fielding said little, but came up to Pennington for a day now and then, rang her youngest child regularly, and made sure Jo went down to Oxfordshire at least once a fortnight.

Since moving into the flat Jo had never felt in the least lonely. But now it had all gone wrong. Her peace was shattered. After a year-long struggle to put Rufus Grierson from her mind he was now all she could think about, including his arbitrary demand to know what happened—or didn't happen—on the date starred in red on her calendar. In the end she thrust the calendar in a drawer and forced herself to ignore it, but the damage to her concentration was done. She switched the computer on every morning, but she was lucky if she managed even a page or two of progress before it was time to pack up for the day and go off to the Mitre.

At the end of the week Jo went early to put flowers on Claire's grave, and stood beside it for some time, staring blindly at the massed blooms heaped on it. Rufus, it seemed, had been earlier still. When she got back she switched on her computer and sat staring at the screen. She was four-fifths of the way through the story, and had only the climax to get in print—the ending which had been planned in her head since the start. But after her early-morning pilgrimage she found it even harder than ever to transfer her finale from her head to the computer, and in the end she gave it up and went out shopping for food supplies.

Later, at the Mitre, where she was working every night for the time being, Jo was too busy to notice when Rufus arrived, unaware that he was watching from the other end of the bar as she poured drinks for a crowd of young men celebrating a stag-night. The prospective bridegroom leaned close, chatting Jo up with a sort of fevered desperation which she parried with her usual impersonal friendliness as she provided him with a tray-load of drinks. She thanked him pleasantly for the large tip he gave her, then turned away to put the money in the staff box, her smile fading as she saw Rufus.

'Hello,' he said quietly.

'Hi.' She summoned the smile back hastily. 'What can I get you? Scotch?'

He nodded, and Jo put a glass up to the optic for a measure of whisky, added some soda and pushed the glass across the bar. Rufus gave her some money and Jo rang it up on the till, feeling tongue-tied.

'How are you?' he asked.

Aware that the query was no automatic, meaningless pleasantry, Jo shrugged. 'I'm fine.'

'When do you finish tonight, Jo?'

'It depends. It was after midnight last night.'

'I'll drive you home.'

'No need; I came on my bike.'

'You really shouldn't ride home alone at that hour,' he said disapprovingly.

Jo's eyes flashed. 'I've been doing it for years. It never worried you before.'

'Because I wasn't aware of it. Now I am. And the risk involved appals me.'

'I cycle along well-lit roads,' she said impatiently, then her eyes narrowed. 'Or are we discussing a different kind of risk here?'

He frowned. 'What do you mean?'

'Oh come *on*,' she said scornfully. 'If the—the eventuality we discussed does occur, you probably think that cycling on a mountain bike isn't a good idea.'

Rufus, to her surprise, looked discomfited. 'I hadn't given it a thought. I was thinking of mugging. Or worse.'

'Oh.' Jo eyed him for a moment, then turned away to serve a sudden influx of customers. When she was free again Rufus was nowhere in sight.

The night seemed long. Normally when she was busy the hours flew by, but after talking to Rufus the time dragged. She was glad when Phil Dexter told her to go home.

'You look tired,' he told her. 'When the other girls get back take some time off, Jo. You've earned it.'

'Thanks. I'll take you up on that.'

When Jo went out into the car park she didn't even bother to fetch her bicycle. Rufus, as expected, was leaning against his car under the exit light, waiting for her. As she drew near he opened the door and Jo slid inside, secretly not sorry to give her cycle ride a miss.

'Have you eaten today?' he asked.

'I had some lunch.'

'Will you scream blue murder if I take you to my place and give you supper?' he asked.

She shook her head, resigned. 'No. Because I know why.'

He shot a sidelong look at her. 'Do you?'

'Today's a year since the funeral. Another anniversary.'

'Actually it's not. You're a day out, Jo.'

'What?' She stared at his profile angrily. 'What are you talking about? Today's the thirtieth of August— a year since Claire was buried. I put flowers on her grave this morning.'

'Didn't you think it strange there were so many there already?' he said gently.

Her eyelids flickered. 'Well—no. I assumed you'd been there early—the Beaumonts too.'

'They're on a cruise. I put the flowers there for them. Yesterday. It's August the thirty-first today, Jo.'

She slumped in her seat, feeling utterly horrified. 'It can't be.'

'It is.'

'Then I missed visiting Claire on the actual day—' She tensed as he put out a hand to grasp hers.

'She's not there, Jo.'

'No.' She breathed in shakily. 'But neither was I. I can't see how I missed it. I stared at that wretched calendar so much I had to put it in a drawer...' She eyed him belligerently. 'You're not joking, Rufus?'

'Of course I'm not joking,' he said with distaste. 'You'd made two marks for the thirtieth, Jo, and only one of them was for Claire's funeral. You've mislaid a day somewhere.'

'I can't imagine how,' she said bitterly. 'It's been the longest week of my life as it is.' She bit her lip. 'I'm not working my usual shifts at the Mitre. I've somehow got out of rhythm.' Heat rose in her face then drained away, leaving her cold, and she trembled as she faced the significance of her discovery. But it was only one day. One day didn't count.

Rufus drew up outside a house halfway along a crescent of the type that Pennington was famed for. Built in the early nineteenth century, with wrought-iron balconies and multi-paned windows breaking the perfect symmetry of the flat, white-painted walls, the house had one of the best addresses in the town.

'I'm surprised you moved here,' she said. 'I thought you preferred the country.'

He helped her out of the car. 'No. It was Claire who wanted to live so far out. Because of her riding. My own preference has always been for a house near the hub of things. But this type rarely comes up for sale. It was in crying need of repair, which meant the price was too tempting to pass up. I've been having it done up for the past six months. It's not finished, by any means, but the roof's secure and the ground floor's habitable.' He led her up the steps to a very handsome front door.

Jo braced herself for the ordeal of confronting Claire's possessions, then paused in the long, narrow hallway in surprise. There was nothing of Claire here. Claire had liked deep-piled, wall-to-wall carpeting, and velvet curtains, with cushions piled on chintz-covered furniture, and ornaments and vases of flowers everywhere. And the house Rufus had bought her had been modern, with big, open-plan rooms and great plate-glass windows.

This house was austere by comparison. The hall floor had no carpet at all to hide black and white diamond-shaped tiles. Delicate wrought-iron banisters edged a stairway which curved up to the first floor with no visible means of support, leaving an alcove below for a pembroke table surmounted by a mirror, both of them new to Jo, who had known Rufus Grierson's former home far better than she knew Rufus.

He ushered her into a sitting room with walls painted the authentic dark red of the Regency period. Several chairs and a large sofa were covered in plain, unbleached linen; heavy straw-coloured silk hung at the tall windows. Books lined white-painted shelves in deep alcoves which flanked the fireplace, and the fringed carpet on the gleaming wood floor was thin and old and obviously hailed from somewhere in the East.

'Do you like it?' asked Rufus.

'Yes. It's lovely,' said Jo faintly.

'The dining room's in here.' He led her along the hall to the next room, where the walls were painted tawny gold, but the only furniture was an oval table with graceful legs ending in brass lion's paws. 'I haven't found the right chairs yet, or some form of sideboard,' he told her, then went ahead of her through an archway into a lofty, spacious kitchen with dark green walls and white cupboards. White wooden shutters were folded back from tall, uncurtained windows, and a door led into a conservatory looking out on a narrow, high-walled garden. Ladder-back chairs surrounded an oak table, and on one of the cupboards a tray waited, laid with coffee-pot and cups.

Rufus pulled out a chair for her. 'Sit down, Jo. I'll make us some sandwiches.'

She did as he said, glad to rest her aching feet. 'What happened to Claire's things?' she asked.

'Are you shocked because I haven't kept them?' He filled a kettle and switched it on, took bread from a crock and began to slice it while Jo thought it over.

'No,' she said at last. 'I think you're very wise. But, my goodness, Rufus, you really loved her, didn't you?'

Rufus turned sharply, his eyes searching. 'Did you ever doubt that?'

'No, never.' She turned away. 'I meant because you let her furnish the other house so completely to her own taste. She wouldn't have liked this at all.'

'I know. Claire wanted something modern, very different from the house she'd been brought up in. So I bought her dream house for her and let her do her own thing with it. And the result was supreme comfort and warmth.' He turned back to make coffee as the kettle boiled.

'Claire loved it—so you were happy.'

'Because she was,' agreed Rufus. He laid smoked salmon on thinly sliced brown bread, added a squeeze of lemon, and cut the sandwiches into neat triangles, then put them on a china platter that Jo had never seen before. 'All her life Claire was surrounded with people wanting to make her happy. You included.'

'I never thought of it that way.'

'You gave in when she wanted you for a bridesmaid.' He put two plates on the table, put the tray in front of her, then sat down opposite her, raising a dark eyebrow at her. 'I knew you weren't keen on the idea.'

She gazed at him in surprise. 'How?'

'Claire told me.' His smile was sardonic. 'Besides, I remember you clearly at the wedding. You didn't enjoy it. But you hid your feelings very well behind those remarkable eyelashes.'

Jo swallowed, deeply thankful that she had. And she knew perfectly well she had long eyelashes, like all the Fielding women. As a student she'd laid on mascara with a lavish hand to emphasise the grey-green eyes she looked on as her only good point. She'd had plenty of compliments on the subject before, but from Rufus it flustered her.

'I couldn't refuse Claire,' she said at last.

'Of course not. No one ever denied Claire anything she wanted in her entire life. Mainly,' added Rufus, 'because she was oddly undemanding. The luxuries in life had always been there for her. She rarely had to ask for anything. It's a miracle she remained so unspoilt.' He pushed the platter towards her. 'Have a sandwich. Sorry it isn't something more exciting, but cooking's not my strong point. How about you?'

'Strictly a no-nonsense cook.' Jo bit into a sandwich without enthusiasm. Normally she loved smoked salmon. But not tonight. She frowned suddenly. 'How did you know I liked this? Claire loathed it.'

Rufus finished his own sandwich unhurriedly, eyeing her with an odd glint of irony. 'I know a lot about you, because Claire kept me fully informed. For instance, I know you're fiercely independent, that you would never accept costly presents from her, or let her treat you to expensive meals, that you were madly in love with someone at university—'

'Good heavens, she told you all that? How boring for you.'

'Not at all. Claire didn't tell me everything at once. Odd snippets of information filtered through from time to time. So before I asked you back tonight I had some smoked salmon in because I remembered it was your favourite.' He smiled. 'The mind is a very complicated piece of machinery.'

So is the body, thought Jo morosely. She eyed the coffee longingly, wondering if it would bring on another headache, or at the very least keep her awake half the night.

'It's decaffeinated,' said Rufus, reading her mind with disquieting ease. 'I remembered the headache.'

'What it is to own a trained legal mind.' Jo smiled a little, and filled the cups, adding milk to her own. 'Would I be trespassing if I asked what you've done with the furniture from the other house?'

'Not at all. I sold most of it at auction.' He shot a dark, remorseful look at her. 'I'm sorry, Jo. Would you have liked anything? It never occurred to me that you would.'

'And you're right,' said Jo swiftly. 'Besides, you gave me the earrings. Or was that Mrs Beaumont's idea?'

'No. It was mine.' He stared down into his coffee-cup. 'Unlike the bridal bouquet on the coffin. That was definitely Gloria's idea.'

Jo nodded, unsurprised. 'I thought it was out of character for you at the time.'

'Gloria thought it was a touch Claire would have loved,' he said without expression.

'She was right.' Jo smiled compassionately. 'But you know that, of course.'

'This is very relaxing,' he said, surprising her. 'With anyone else it would be treason to admit that sometimes Claire and I saw things in a different light.'

'But isn't that what loving someone means? Accepting the differences?' asked Jo carefully. 'Claire and I were poles apart in so many ways it was a miracle we stayed so close. She was so lovely through and through, it was hard to live up to her sometimes.' She smiled wryly. 'I knew that my lifestyle was anathema to her. To be honest, hers was to me too, but it made no difference.'

'You're an unusual lady, Jo Fielding. Have another sandwich.' Rufus offered the platter, but she shook her head, wondering what he meant by 'unusual'.

'I'm sorry, Rufus, after you took the trouble to make them, but I'm really not hungry.'

'Because you're too damn tired to eat,' he said forcefully, and pushed the plate away. 'Do you have to work behind that bar so much?'

'Actually, I don't have to work there at all, if you mean from a financial point of view.'

He propped his elbows on the table and leaned his chin on his hands, eyeing her intently. 'Then your freelancing is actually profitable?'

'Profitable enough to feed me, certainly. But even if I get my book published I'll probably still put in an hour or two at the Mitre because I like the contact with other people.' She sobered abruptly. 'Unless fate conspires against me, of course.'

Rufus reached across the table and took her hand. 'Cross that bridge when you come to it, as my mother's fond of saying.'

'So's mine.' Jo managed a smile. 'How *is* your mother? I used to see her quite often at Claire's—I mean your place—the other house—'

'I know what you mean,' he said, amused. 'And my mother's very well. She's away with my father, walking in the Trossachs—part of her new health regime for him. Father's threatening to come out of retirement to get some peace.'

Jo chuckled. 'If your mother intends him to get fit he'd better resign himself to it first as last.'

'Exactly what I told him. Mother's a very determined lady. She likes you,' he added casually. 'She asked me quite recently how you were. I had to admit I didn't know. She gave me rather a tongue-lashing on the subject.'

'Goodness! Is that why you came to see me?' Jo's teasing smile faded as she met the look in Rufus' eyes.

'You know it wasn't. I came that night because you were the one person in the world I could talk to.' His eyes held hers. 'I never meant to do more than talk, Jo. You must believe that.'

She breathed in shakily, and removed her hand. 'Oh, I do. With no difficulty at all. I know perfectly well I'm not your type—any more than you're mine.' Which was such a downright lie that she looked away hurriedly.

'What's "type" got to do with it? You're very attractive, Jo Fielding. More cerebral than Claire in one way, and yet a lot more earthy in another. And that's the last comparison I ever intend to make on the subject,' he added emphatically, and raised a sardonic eyebrow. 'I'm not alone in my opinion of your charms, am I? Earlier on, the prospective bridegroom forgot his approaching obligations when he saw you. He could hardly tear himself away from the bar all evening.'

Jo looked at him in surprise. 'I thought you'd gone.'

'I just went into the other bar and did the crossword. I could see you from where I sat.'

'You were checking up on me?' she said, scowling.

'No. Just making sure the drunken bridegroom gave you no real hassle.'

'What would you have done if he had?'

'Shown him the error of his ways.'

'I might have welcomed his attentions, for all you know.'

'I seriously doubt it.'

He was dead right on that score, thought Jo. With Rufus in the vicinity all other men paled into insignificance. She stood up, suddenly brisk. 'I really must go home. I'm not used to working every night. I'm tired.'

Rufus got up. 'Stay in bed as long as possible in the morning.'

'If I do that the newsagent will run out of my favourite Sunday paper,' she said, yawning as they went along the austerely elegant hall.

Rufus paused before opening the door. 'I'll buy it for you and bring it round after midday. Then you can lie in as long as you want.'

Jo was tempted. Then she remembered that all this attention from Rufus was for a very specific reason. 'That's very kind of you, but the shop doesn't open until ten. And that's quite long enough to stay in bed. Even on my day off.'

Rufus shrugged, and during the journey home told her about his brother's forthcoming wedding. 'My parents will be back long before then, of course. Mother bought her outfit ages ago, so she could wear it in the evenings at the hotel in Scotland.'

Jo laughed. 'Practical lady, your mother.'

'I've got a secret suspicion that only care for my feelings prevented her from attending Rory's wedding in the outfit bought for mine,' he said drily.

'Would you have minded if she had?'

'To be honest I can't remember it.'

Because he'd had eyes only for Claire that day, thought Jo, downcast, and got out of the car. Rufus accompanied her to the door, waiting until she'd unlocked it.

'Jo, you'd be doing me a very great service if you came to Rory's wedding with me,' he said casually.

She stared up at him, aghast. 'You're joking!'

'I'm not. In the light of our previous connection no one would think it odd if I took you as my guest.'

'*I* would,' she said bluntly. 'Sorry, Rufus. Nothing doing.'

'Not even to rescue me from Susannah's endless matchmaking? Rory tipped me off that one of her unattached friends has been invited to partner me.'

'You're more than capable of dealing with the situation!' Jo assured him tartly.

'Think it over,' he said casually. 'You may change your mind. Goodnight.'

CHAPTER FOUR

To HER secret regret Jo heard no more from Rufus for several days, each of which grew longer and less bearable. Her concentration deteriorated to the point of non-existence, and because she was back to her normal routine of three evenings a week at the Mitre even the noise and diversion there was denied her some days. By mid-week Jo could stand it no longer. She bought a pregnancy-testing kit and confirmed what she'd known, in her heart of hearts, all along. Horrified, she made an appointment with her doctor, but the official test, just like her own, was obdurately positive.

When she reported for work on Friday evening she asked Phil Dexter if she could take the next week off as he'd mentioned, and he agreed promptly, telling her to take a fortnight. Jo thanked him warmly and turned away to serve a customer, and almost at once the usual pre-dinner rush began, with no sign of Rufus, and very little time to think of him or her predicament. It was almost nine, and all the diners had departed for the restaurant, effecting the usual mid-evening lull, when Jo saw Rufus come in and make straight for the bar.

'Hello,' he said, settling on a stool.

'Hi,' said Jo, trying to hide her delight at the sight of him. 'What can I get you?'

'Just a beer tonight.'

'Not your usual tipple,' she commented, filling a pint glass.

'I can make beer last longer than whisky, which makes my presence easier to account for while I wait for you,' he informed her.

Jo looked at him levelly as he handed her the money for the drink. 'You needn't, Rufus. I know my way home.'

'Nevertheless, I'll drive you.' He eyed her searchingly as she handed him the change. 'Sleeping badly?'

'Yes,' she muttered, glad when a new influx of customers made further conversation impossible, and Rufus retired to a corner to read his paper.

To her surprise half an hour later Phil Dexter handed her a paypacket and told her to go home. 'One of Louise's girls is coming to give us a hand. You look done in, Jo. Enjoy your holiday.'

'Thanks, Phil.' She smiled at him gratefully. 'I'll collect my bike tomorrow. I've got a lift home.'

He nodded, grinning. 'I thought so. That's why I'm letting you off early. Regular little fairy godfather, that's me.'

Jo chuckled. 'Thanks, Phil. Goodnight.' She collected her jacket and glanced across the crowded room at Rufus, who rose to his feet and followed her outside to the car park.

'You're early tonight,' he commented.

'Dispensation from the boss.'

'Good.' He looked down into her face as he helped her into the car. 'You look tired.'

Jo shrugged. 'Busy night.'

'Let's go back to my place—'

'I'd rather go straight home.' She eyed his profile diffidently as he got in beside her. 'Would you care to come in for a while?'

He shot a look at her. 'Of course I would.'

Neither of them made any attempt at conversation on the short journey to Bruton Road. Jo unlocked the door and went upstairs ahead of Rufus, and only broke the silence when she asked him to sit down once they were inside the flat.

'I've got some beer, or there's the remains of the brandy,' she said nervously as he remained on his feet.

Rufus looked down at her, one eyebrow raised. 'Why don't *you* sit down and I'll get the drinks?'

Jo shook her head. 'Actually, I'm rather hungry. Have you had dinner?'

'No. I had a long, boring lunch with one of my clients today.' Rufus shrugged. 'I was going to put something together for us at my place. Not that it was a success last time. You hardly ate anything.'

'To be honest—' she began, then stopped as he winced. 'What's the matter?'

'I tend to duck when you say that.'

'I was just going to say I'm not used to one-to-one situations with you, Rufus.' Her eyes gleamed pale in her sun-darkened face. 'Last time it acted like an appetite suppressant! But tonight I'm hungry. How about an omelette?'

'Perfect. What can I do?'

'Help yourself to a drink while I cook. It won't take long. The beer's in the fridge.'

He looked round. 'I'll pass on that for the moment. Coffee, maybe, after the omelette?'

Jo had been modest when she'd described herself as a no-nonsense cook. The sizzling, golden creation she handed Rufus ten minutes later was fragrant with herbs grown in her own window-boxes. He accepted it with mock reverence, and obeyed with alacrity when told to get on with it while the chef cooked her own. Accompanied by crisp rolls from the nearby bakery, followed by an apple for Jo and some deliquescent Brie for Rufus, the meal was eaten with despatch while they discussed items in the news that day.

Afterwards Jo refused Rufus' half-hearted offer of help and took the dishes into the kitchen, returning afterwards with two mugs of coffee.

'Instant and decaffeinated,' she said without apology, and gave him a wry smile.

'What is it?'

'I was just thinking how wonderfully civilised we are.'

'Conversing politely, even though you invited me solely to answer the question I'm burning to ask,' he said promptly.

'You're a clever devil, Rufus,' she allowed. 'In some ways it's surprising you were attracted to Claire. She would have been the first to admit she wasn't academic.'

'I was drawn to her for the same reason you were her life-long friend—the attraction of opposites.' He leaned back in his chair, watching her closely with dark, half-veiled eyes.

'I didn't mean anything derogatory,' said Jo hastily.

'I know you didn't. You and I, Jo Fielding, are very alike in some ways.' He smiled at her scathing look of disbelief. 'Oh, yes, we are. I follow your thought processes with surprising ease on occasion.'

Since Jo couldn't deny this she took refuge in sarcasm. 'I certainly can't follow yours. Except in this instance. You want to know if I'm pregnant, and I'm forced to own up that I am. The doctor confirmed it this morning.'

Rufus received the news without noticeable re-action, other than a moment or two of silence while he digested it. 'Strange, isn't it?' he said at last. 'I tried for two years to father a child for Claire and failed—'

'But just one encounter with me and bingo!' said Jo bitterly. 'At least you now know you weren't to blame before.'

'I knew that early on,' he informed her. 'Tests were done on both of us.'

'Oh.' Jo felt her colour rise, and Rufus leaned forward to take her hands.

'So let's discuss what happens next.'

She frowned. 'What do you mean? Nothing happens next. Not until May of next year.'

His grasp tightened. 'You obviously haven't thought this through—'

'You have to be joking!' she ripped at him, and yanked her hands away. 'I've done nothing else but think since the moment you brought the subject of pregnancy up. Odd, really. Usually something you dread so much turns out better than you expected or doesn't happen at all. But not this time.' Jo's eyes flashed at him like an angry cat's. 'Claire was the one who wanted a child, remember.'

'I'm hardly likely to forget!' He breathed in deeply. 'Look, Jo, apologies are useless now the damage is done. All I can do is try to put things right—'

'Don't dare offer me money,' she interrupted fiercely.

Rufus glared at her. 'I wasn't about to!'

Jo jumped to her feet. 'In that case, now you've had your question answered it's time you went. I'm tired.'

'Sit down,' said Rufus, without emphasis.

She looked at him for a moment, then resumed her chair.

'I'm offering something quite different,' he went on. 'As I said before, I would very much like a child. And I would prefer that child to have a father married to his mother. Are you with me so far, Jo?'

'I certainly am not,' she lied, secretly ravished by the idea. 'Are you mad?'

'No. My thought processes are functioning normally,' he returned, unmoved. 'Try setting your own in motion. We marry quietly, as soon after my brother's wedding as possible, and you move in with me—purely to keep up appearances, if you prefer it that way.'

'I don't,' wailed Jo, horrified at the prospect of Rufus forced into marriage with her. 'I've no intention of moving from here—'

'You don't have to. Keep this as a bolt-hole of your own, a place for writing your novel.'

Jo shook her head emphatically. 'Look, Rufus, you don't have to marry me just because you made me pregnant by accident. It's very—very civil of you, and I appreciate the offer, but these days it isn't in the least necessary.'

His mouth tightened. 'It is for me.'

She thrust a hand through her hair. 'Rufus, what exactly are we discussing here? Are you suggesting I marry you, give birth to my baby in due course then hand her over to you and take myself off out of her life?'

He smiled faintly. 'You said "my baby", so I know there's no possibility of that. You merely share a house with me and carry on with your writing. I could run to a nanny—'

'Stop!' Jo held up her hand. 'You're going too fast. We're overlooking a couple of details, Rufus.'

'Go on.'

Her eyes fell. 'There's Claire, for a start.'

A shadow darkened Rufus' face. 'Do you imagine I haven't *been* thinking of her? But she wouldn't want either of us to go on mourning for ever, Jo.'

'No. But she wouldn't expect us to get married either. At least, not to each other.'

'What makes you say that?'

'Because you and I disliked each other, for a start.'

Rufus leaned over and took her hand again. 'You used the past tense, Jo.'

She looked up, startled. 'Did I?'

'What other objection would Claire have?' said Rufus.

'The baby.' Jo sighed heavily. 'If the situations were reversed and I was the wife who'd died, I'd be so jealous, I'd come back and haunt you.'

'Claire would never do that,' he said with certainty.

'I know, I know! Which is why you can't want to marry me, Rufus. I'm just not up to Claire's standard. I'm not serene and good-tempered and loving like she was—'

'No. You're not. The contrast couldn't be more marked,' he agreed, to her annoyance. 'That's why the arrangement will work.' He got up, pulling her to her feet with him. 'I'll say no more tonight. Sleep on it, and we'll talk again tomorrow. I'll call round at about half-seven and take you out to dinner.'

Jo opened her mouth to refuse, then closed it again. Why not? She had nothing else to do. 'All right. But not to the Mitre, please.'

'Give me credit for more tact than that,' he said drily, and raised her face to his with the tip of one finger. 'Jo, it was never my intention to turn your life upside down. But, having done so, I intend to put it right as far as I can. Have you told your mother yet?'

'No,' said Jo miserably.

'Good. Because when you do don't ring her. We'll drive down and tell her together.'

'But you can't do that! I haven't agreed to marry you yet.'

'Whether you do or not, I shall give her an edited version of what happened. The least I can do is to make matters clear to her,' he said emphatically.

'Mother will find it hard to believe!'

'That you're expecting a baby, or that I'm the father?' he said, with a crooked smile.

Unwillingly Jo smiled back. 'Oh, the last bit, definitely. On the first bit she'll be euphoric. Thalia and Callie are dragging their heels a bit about babies.'

To her infinite surprise Rufus took her in his arms and held her in a loose, comforting embrace. 'Go to bed, Jo. Don't think about this any more tonight. Just sleep. I'll see you tomorrow night.' He released her and stood back. 'Thanks for the omelette—the best I've ever tasted.'

Jo managed a smile as she saw him to the door. 'You should taste my chicken cacciatora!'

'Any time you say!' he said promptly. 'Good night, Jo. Sleep well.'

* * *

Fully expecting to lie awake all night, Jo slept from the moment she went to bed until after nine the next morning. When she woke she lay still for a long time, coming to terms with the fact that her mind had made itself up while she was sleeping. She would be a fool to turn down Rufus as a husband, whatever the circumstances. She would never love anyone else. And in time he might come to care for her in return. Not as he'd done for Claire, of course, but enough for a good marriage just the same.

Hard on the heels of this discovery came another— her muse was back with her in full force, words crowding into her mind with such insistence that Jo jumped out of bed and washed and dressed at top speed. Pausing only to swallow some cereal, she patted her stomach apologetically then took her cup of tea to her desk and sat down with anticipation at her computer.

Jo worked all day, stopping only for an occasional cup of coffee, plus a sandwich at lunchtime. Words flowed from her brain to the screen with such fluency that it was as if someone else were dictating the story. Only superhuman self-control made her switch off the computer in time to take a bath and get ready for Rufus.

When he arrived, exactly at seven-thirty, Jo's hair was gleaming and her face made up with care, but she was still in her dressing gown.

'Hi,' she said, as she let him in, taking in his lightweight suit. 'I'm ready except for the choice of clothes. I forgot to ask where you were taking me.'

'I booked a table at the Chesterton,' he said, eyeing her closely. 'You look a lot better today, Jo. Did you sleep?'

'Like a log,' she assured him. 'Have a drink, or read the paper—I shan't be long.'

Autumn was in the air, but the evening was sunny, and after a moment's hesitation Jo took down the dress her mother had given her for her birthday. At first Jo had baulked at the price of it, but in the end, entranced by the brief, sixties-style shift in leaf-green wool crêpe, she gave in. And tonight was a good night to wear it. Another month or so and she'd have a fight to get into it. She slid her feet into low-heeled leather sling-backs, renewed her lipstick and went into the other room to join Rufus. He threw down the book he was reading and jumped to his feet.

'Jo!' His eyes moved over her with appreciation. 'You look wonderful. Where did you find a dress to match your eyes so exactly?'

'My eyes are very accommodating. They change from grey to green and back again, according to what I wear—and how I feel,' she added deliberately.

Rufus moved nearer. 'Do I take it you feel well to-night, then?'

'Better, certainly.' She smiled at him, her eyes glittering with satisfaction. 'I wrote five thousand words or so today, Rufus. The muse came back.'

His eyes narrowed. 'Had it deserted you?'

She nodded. 'I was worried. I thought it had gone for good. I had the ending for my book all ready in my head, but I just couldn't get it *out* of my head and into the computer. Then this morning I woke up and the muse was there, prodding me out of bed to get started.'

The evening got off to a good start and improved as the hours passed. There was a moment when Jo wanted to hang back as they reached the Chesterton, reluctant to walk into a restaurant full of people who knew Rufus as Claire's husband. But to her relief there were no familiar faces in the room when the *maître d'hôtel* called them in from the bar to their first course.

She confessed her diffidence to Rufus over crab ravioli.

'Would it matter to you so much, then?' he asked, pouring local spring water into her glass.

'Yes, I think so.' She looked him in the eye. 'I still feel guilty, Rufus.'

'If anyone should feel guilty it's me, not you, Jo,' he said firmly. 'And, as it happens, I rarely came here with Claire. She liked to drive into the country to eat.'

'I remember. The Blue Boar was one of her favourites.'

'Jo, let's not talk about Claire.'

She laid down her fork and looked at him searchingly. 'Does it still hurt so much, then?'

His eyes shuttered. 'Lately, to be honest, it doesn't. Since the night I came to your flat, to be specific.' Rufus smiled. 'You're blushing, Jo.'

'As well I might,' she muttered, swallowing some water hastily.

'It wasn't the first time I'd felt like contacting you. I've wanted to get in touch often during the past year.'

'Why didn't you, then?'

'Gloria Beaumont insisted you were about to get married. It seemed callous to spoil things for you by reopening old wounds. And,' Rufus added bluntly, 'I knew damn well you didn't like me.'

She bit her lip. 'You didn't like me either.'

'It seems hard to remember that at this particular moment in time,' he said drily.

A waiter came to remove their plates, and they were halfway through the main course before Rufus returned to the subject.

'What I'm trying to say is that after I made love to you I felt as though a great cloud had lifted from my life.' His eyes met hers across the table, which was in a secluded corner, far enough away from the nearest diners to give them privacy. 'Sounds insane, put into words.'

'Not to me, because in some ways I felt the same. Until I realised there would be a sequel to the story!' Jo smiled at him crookedly. 'You've probably gathered that I intend to take you up on your offer.'

Rufus laid down his knife and fork, his eyes holding hers. 'You mean that?'

'Yes,' she said simply.

'You've obviously given it some thought.'

'Strangely enough, no. I went straight to sleep last night, and when I woke up this morning my mind had made itself up during the night. Marrying you seemed the logical thing to do—under the circumstances,' she added deliberately. 'Otherwise, Rufus, marrying the still grieving widower of my best friend would not be a tempting prospect. But you want a child, and I'm going to give birth to yours whether I want to or not, so the only sensible thing to do is accept your offer.' Sensible, possibly, but whether it was wise where only one partner loved the other was open to debate, thought Jo with secret misgivings.

'Would you like something else?' asked Rufus abruptly, and when she shook her head he rose to his feet and came round the table. 'Then we'll go home for coffee and start planning.'

Twenty minutes later Jo was sitting at the kitchen table in Beaufort Crescent, facing Rufus Grierson across the coffee-tray he'd laid in readiness before going out.

'You're very organised,' she said as she poured.

'I'm a lawyer, Jo. I'm required to be organised and logical. Which is why getting married seemed the obvious solution to our particular problem. Though I don't look on it as a problem myself. Do you?'

Jo sipped her coffee thoughtfully. 'Not so much now.' She looked around her, then smiled at him mockingly. 'Though I think this house made my mind up for me. The prospect of living here tipped the scales.'

Rufus chuckled. 'Don't speak too soon. Upstairs it's a shambles. I've got as far as having the bathroom refitted, and the main bedroom decorated. But the floors are bare, and the furniture consists solely of a bed and a wardrobe. Before you move in I'll get the other bedrooms sorted out.'

'Can you afford all this?' she asked bluntly. 'Unlike Claire I don't have any money.'

He shrugged. 'I can house and feed you without resort to any money of yours, Jo. The other house took a while to sell, but in the end it fetched a good price due to the refurbished stables. The people who bought it are horse-mad, like Claire.'

Jo eyed him uncomfortably. 'Please don't take offence, Rufus, but was the house yours? I mean, Claire didn't pay for it, did she?'

'No.' He met her eyes squarely. 'Claire had no money of her own, Jo. Her father wanted to settle a lump sum on her when we got married, but I drew the line at that. I staved him off by letting him buy

her a horse, and promising to let him contribute to
school fees at some future date. I could never get
Claire to make a will, but it made very little difference. Her possessions were mostly clothes and
jewellery. I returned the latter to the Beaumonts, along
with the china and crystal they gave us as wedding
presents. I kept the silver from my parents, and sent
Claire's clothes to charity shops.

'The house, and everything in it,' he said with emphasis, 'is mine. So no hang-ups, Jo. It's time to get
on with our lives. Once Rory's wedding is over we'll
announce ours.' He reached over and took Jo's hand.
'But let's keep the baby to ourselves for a while, except
for your mother.'

'Surely you'll tell your own mother?'

'In time. Let's live with the idea for a while ourselves first.' The overhead light burnished his hair with
silver as he leaned nearer, his grasp tightening. 'Do
you still hate the thought of motherhood, Jo?'

She thought it over. 'I never *hated* the idea, exactly.
But it was Claire who always wanted babies. The only
thing I ever burned to produce was my brainchild—
my novel. Lots of women bring up children single-
handed and make a fantastic job of it, but I never
had ambitions to do the same.' She looked at him
candidly. 'I panicked at first.'

Rufus smiled. 'Have you stopped panicking now?'

'About the baby, yes.' Jo bit her lip. 'About marrying you, I'm not so sure. It still hasn't sunk in. And
you haven't tried living with me yet. I can be difficult
in creative mode.'

'At which point you can retreat to your attic,' he
said, unmoved. 'But we're two intelligent adults, Jo.

We should be able to occupy the same house without coming to blows.'

'I'm very sure of that,' she assured him. 'Never in my wildest dreams could I picture you letting fly with your fists.'

'Not where a woman's concerned, certainly.' Rufus released her hand and took a diary from his pocket. 'Now let's get down to business and settle a date. I suggest we get married three weeks from now, and Mother can wear the same gear she bought for Rory's wedding.'

Jo stared at him, startled. 'That soon?'

'I think we should put things in motion as quickly as possible,' he said matter-of-factly. 'And if anyone's overcome by the surprise factor we'll imply that it's not as sudden as it seems, but you insisted on waiting until a year had elapsed after Claire died.'

'You've got it all worked out to the last detail, Rufus,' she said drily. 'What would you have done if I'd refused to marry you after all?'

'Kept persuading until you gave in.'

'The child is that important to you?'

'Now there's the actual possibility of one, yes.' He held out his hand. 'Come on, I'll take you home; you need your sleep.'

Her eyes narrowed. 'You're not going to nag a lot, are you, Rufus?'

'Nag?' he said with distaste.

'Over whether I eat the right things, and behave like a sensible mother-to-be.' Jo eyed him militantly. 'I'm used to pleasing myself. If we live together—'

'When,' he corrected her.

'All right, *when* we live together you'll have to give me space. I've lived alone for the past six months and

I've loved it.' She sighed. 'I hadn't expected to give it up so soon.'

Rufus sat down again. 'I know I vetoed more comparisons, but one thing I should make clear, if only for your peace of mind, Jo, is that I value time to myself as much as you do. Claire could never understand that. Solitude frightened her.'

'I know.' Jo's eyes darkened. 'That's why I was so glad she died instantly. She never had time to be frightened of what came next.'

Rufus jumped up and pulled her out of her chair and into his arms, holding her in a firm, impersonal embrace.

'It's all right,' she said, her voice muffled against his chest. 'I'm not going to cry again.'

He made no move to relax his hold and Jo leaned against him for a while, taking comfort in his nearness before a warning voice reminded her of what had happened the last time Rufus Grierson took her in his arms. She moved, and his arms fell away, and when she looked up at him she found his eyes smiling down into hers with amused comprehension. 'Don't worry, Jo. I shan't take advantage of the new arrangement.'

She coloured. 'No. I'm sure you won't.'

'Which,' he went on blandly, 'doesn't mean I wouldn't like to. I'm just a human male animal like any other man, Miss Fielding.'

'Tell me about it!' she said tartly. 'Why else are we landed in this situation?'

He gave her a most un-Rufus-like grin, and gave her a deliberately chaste kiss on the cheek. 'Don't worry. I keep that side of me under wraps ninety-nine per cent of the time.'

CHAPTER FIVE

Jo FOUND that her agreement to marry Rufus set the ball rolling with a vengeance.

'Mother,' she said on the phone next morning, after the usual chat, 'will the roast stretch to an extra guest for lunch today?'

'Of course, darling. Who are you bringing?'

'Rufus Grierson,' said Jo baldly, with no attempt to break the news more subtly.

There was silence on the other end of the line for a moment. 'You do mean Claire's husband?' said Rose Fielding after a while.

'How many Rufus Griersons do I know?'

'Don't be flippant! You can't blame me for wondering why you're bringing him to lunch. He's never been a favourite with you.'

Jo blushed, unseen. 'Well, things have changed a bit. We've been seeing each other lately.'

'Good heavens—you never mentioned it!'

'No, I know. But I'm mentioning it now, so is it all right to bring him?'

'Of course. Shall I ask Thalia and Charles too?'

'*No!* Just the three of us—please.'

After a few minutes' conversation to report her progress with her book Jo rang off and dialled Rufus' number. 'Permission granted.'

'Good. How are you this morning?'

'Fine. How are you?'

'Relieved.'

'Because I said yes?'

'Yes.'

'Not a man to waste words, are you?' she said drily.

'If you wish me to wax flowery, I will,' he assured her.

'Perish the thought! Just collect me at eleven—please.'

When Rufus arrived Jo went downstairs to join him, wearing her jade-green shirt with cream linen trousers and a fawn cotton cable-knit sweater knotted round her shoulders—an outfit carefully chosen to show up her tan.

'Hi,' she said, smiling at Rufus, who, to her surprise, bent to kiss her cheek.

'In case the neighbours are watching,' he said suavely as he held the car door open for her. 'You look good this morning.'

'I feel fine.' She looked at him as he slid in beside her. 'You look good too.'

'I aim to please,' he said drily.

And, in her case, succeeded, always, thought Jo. Rufus Grierson managed, without effort, to look elegant whatever he wore, and today was no exception. His grey trousers were in a Prince of Wales check that only legs as long as his could carry off, worn with a shirt in a lighter shade of silver-grey. A matching jacket lay on the back seat with a silk tie tucked in the pocket.

'I opted for a suit under the circumstances,' he informed her. 'I shall put the jacket on before we arrive to impress your mother.'

He probably would impress her, too, thought Jo. 'I'm a bit nervous,' she confessed. 'Mother was very surprised when I asked to bring you to lunch.'

'How will she take our news, do you think?'

'Rufus, I haven't a clue. My mother's never predictable.' Jo shrugged. 'But, whatever her reaction, it won't make any difference.'

'You mean her disapproval won't change your mind?'

'Right. When I make promises I keep them.'

'Good.' He put a hand over hers for a moment. 'I've got a bottle of Bollinger and some flowers in the boot.'

'Goodness. She'll definitely be impressed.'

Rose Fielding, wearing a dark green dress to complement eyes like her daughter's, came out of the lodge to greet them as Rufus nosed the car through the imposing gates to Willowdene Manor. She kissed her daughter, then turned to Rufus, who by this time was formal in jacket and tie.

'This is quite a surprise,' she said frankly, holding out her hand. 'How are you, Rufus? We haven't met since your wedding.'

Not one to beat about the bush, her mother, thought Jo.

'I'm a lot better now than I've been in a long time, Mrs Fielding,' said Rufus without turning a hair. 'It's very kind of you to put up with an extra lunch guest at such short notice.'

The niceties over, Rose Fielding led them inside her small, compact home, where scents of rosemary and garlic came to greet them from the open kitchen door.

'Sorry about the cooking smells. In my doll's house here one can't keep the menu a secret, I'm afraid,' she said briskly. 'It's all ready, but let's have a drink before we eat.'

Rufus asked for gin and tonic, then excused himself to go out to the car, giving Rose the opportunity to submit her daughter to a searching scrutiny before turning away to mix drinks.

'How long has this been going on, Jo?'

'A while.'

'You haven't brought a man here since you gave Edward his marching orders. Do I take it that you and Rufus are more than just friends?'

'Yes,' said Jo briefly. 'I just want tonic, Mother. No gin.'

Further conversation was prevented by Rufus' reappearance with a sheaf of multicoloured Michaelmas daisies.

Rose Fielding took them with an exclamation of pleasure. 'How very nice of you. I love autumn flowers. These are early because of the heatwave. Thank you, Rufus. I'll go and put them in water. You see to his drink, Jo.'

Rufus raised a questioning eyebrow at Jo as she handed him the glass.

'Leave it until lunch is over,' she whispered.

When Rose came back she'd obviously decided to accept the situation without further comment and chatted easily for a while on events in Pennington before taking them in to eat at the table situated at one end of the kitchen.

'Rather informal, I'm afraid,' said Rose as she waved them to their places. 'They knocked two rooms into one when all the renovations were being done, but I'm quite happy to sacrifice a dining room to a larger kitchen.'

'You chose well,' said Rufus as his hostess served them with clear soup made from her own home-grown tomatoes. 'Wonderful view across the gardens.'

Rufus was gracefully appreciative about the roast lamb he volunteered to carve, and Rose Fielding visibly warmed towards him as she passed round vegetables grown in the small garden at the back of the lodge. They had eaten plum pie, and were drinking coffee in the sitting room when Jo put down her cup and exchanged a look with Rufus, who was sitting on the sofa beside her.

'As you so rightly suspect, Mother,' she began, 'this is no ordinary visit.'

Rose Fielding nodded slowly. 'I'd gathered that.'

'Mrs Fielding, Jo is expecting my child,' said Rufus, taking over. He slid an arm round Jo's waist. 'We're getting married in three weeks' time, and we've come here today to ask your blessing.'

Mrs Fielding sat very still, her eyes wide with shock. 'Good heavens,' she said faintly. She looked from her daughter's vivid, defensive face to the self-contained features of Rufus Grierson as he held Jo closer in unconscious protection. 'No ordinary visit indeed,' she said at last, then held out her arms and Jo flew into them, the knot of tension inside her dissolving at last as her mother held her close.

From that moment on all constraint vanished. Once she'd recovered from the shock of Rufus Grierson as a prospective son-in-law Rose Fielding grew euphoric at the idea of a grandchild. Pleased that she was the only one to share the secret, she promised to keep it to herself for the time being, and after Rufus opened the celebratory champagne the rest of the day went so well that Rose Fielding included Rufus in her embrace when they said their goodbyes.

'Mother accepted the situation more easily than I expected,' said Jo with relief, as they were driving back to Pennington. 'I had my doubts for a while.'

'So did I,' said Rufus, and glanced at her. 'You were alone with your mother before we left. Is she really as pleased as she says?'

'Oh, yes. With Mother what you see is what you get. Which is why things were a bit sticky at first. She couldn't see why, exactly, I'd seen fit to bring Claire's husband to lunch.'

'Jo, we both loved her very much, but it would be better—for both of us—if you tried not to think of me solely as Claire's husband from now on,' said Rufus.

She kept her eyes on the road, saying nothing for a moment. 'Yes,' she said slowly. 'I suppose it would.'

'Is it so difficult to imagine me as *your* husband?' he asked bluntly.

It was the stuff of fantasy to Jo in some ways—the dream she'd never let herself dream. When Rufus stopped the car in Bruton Road she looked at him objectively for a moment. 'It's still hard to believe,' she said with perfect truth.

'It might help if you come to Rory's wedding with me,' he said, and got out of the car before Jo could refuse. 'Since we are now engaged—'

'Committed, not engaged,' she retorted as she unlocked the door. 'Are you coming in for a while?'

'Yes. I need information for form-filling. And I meant what I said about the wedding,' he added as he followed her upstairs. 'My parents are due back tomorrow. I'd rather they, at least, knew straight away, before I put the announcement in the local paper.'

Jo went inside and threw her sweater down on a chair. 'Do we have to go public, Rufus?'

Rufus nodded, then strolled after her to lean in the kitchen doorway, arms folded as he watched her fill a kettle. 'Let's observe the conventions as much as possible.'

Jo looked at him over her shoulder. 'In that case I suppose it would look odd if I didn't go to Rory's wedding.'

'Precisely.' Rufus moved towards her and turned her round. 'But quite apart from that I'd very much *like* you to come with me.'

She looked up at him. 'You know, I take it, why I'm not keen on the idea?'

'Because you haven't been to a wedding since you were bridesmaid to Claire, I imagine.' His eyes held hers. 'This is the first since then for me too.'

Jo gave in. 'All right. I'll come. Now let's have something to eat. I'm hungry.'

He grinned. 'After that enormous lunch you tucked away at your mother's? Where do you put it all?'

'I think the appetite comes with the territory,' she said tartly. 'In popular parlance, Mr Grierson, I'm eating for two.' She turned away and began rummaging in a cupboard. 'I've got some prawns. Do you like those? I could make a salad with the stuff Mother gave me from her garden. And she gave me a fruit-cake too.'

'If I'd thought you were that hungry I'd have taken you for a meal on the way back!'

Jo shook her head as she began washing lettuce. 'No need.' She looked up. 'Unless you'd have preferred that?'

'No, I wouldn't,' he said emphatically. 'You may have difficulties in adjusting to me as your husband, Jo, but it's getting easier every day to imagine you as my wife.'

Sudden heat coursed along Jo's veins, and in confusion she turned away to toss the salad with some of her mother's special dressing. She drained the prawns and added them with an unsteady hand, then sliced a crusty loaf, clumsier than usual because Rufus was watching every move she made.

When they were seated at the table, with the salad bowl and a platter of cheese and bread between them, Jo drew in a deep breath.

'Before we eat there's something I must make clear, Rufus.'

He raised an eyebrow in polite inquiry. 'What is it?'

'You have to give me time to get used to all this.' She coloured. 'I'm not saying—I dislike you. Believe me, I wouldn't even contemplate marrying you if I did, baby or no baby—'

'No need to go on, Jo. You're saying that you've agreed to marry me solely because you're going to be the mother of my child, not from any yen to become my wife.' He helped himself to salad. 'I understand what you're saying. I won't make any rash, male assumptions.'

'Right.' Jo smiled brightly. 'Now what information did you want?'

'Oh, just basic things—full name, date of birth and so on,' he said casually. 'This dressing is superb.'

'Mother's trade secret.'

'I like your mother.'

'Good.' Jo grinned. 'Since she kissed you goodbye today one must assume she reciprocates. Mother's like me—not much into kissing.'

Rufus' eyes dropped to her mouth. 'Pity,' he said lightly. 'Are you fond of leftover salad for breakfast, or may I polish it off?'

After supper Rufus took out a diary and sat, pen poised, while Jo provided him with details of her birth. He wrote them down, then looked up. 'First name. Are you Josephine or Joanna?'

Jo cast her eyes skywards. 'Neither. My father taught classics, remember. I'm Jocasta.'

Rufus whistled. 'Jocasta, no less!' He grinned. 'I don't know why you're so hung up on marrying your friend's husband. Your namesake married her own son!'

'Only by mistake,' she retorted. 'I loved my father dearly, but why Mother let him have his way about naming us I'll never know. The twins are Thalia and Calypso, poor things, but at least Callie and I can shorten ours. You can't do much with Thalia.'

'True. What shall we name ours?'

Jo's eyes widened. 'Glory, I don't know. I hadn't got that far. Something ordinary and unmythical for preference.'

'Do you have another name?'

'No. Jocasta was more than enough.'

Rufus surveyed her lazily. 'I think it suits you. Perhaps I'll call you Jocasta from now on.'

'Then the deal's off,' she said promptly.

'In which case I'll wait until we're legally married.' Rufus got up. 'Are you working much this week?'

'No. I've got a fortnight off.' Jo looked up at him ruefully. 'But under the circumstances I suppose I'd better tell Phil I'm not going back at all.'

Rufus reached down and pulled her to her feet. 'I'm glad you came to that decision by yourself. It's been occupying my mind rather a lot.'

She smiled. 'How forbearing of you not to pressurise me! But I'm not sorry to give it up. Now I've got the bit between my teeth I want to finish this book before we get married if I can.'

'Good. I draw the line at a computer in the luggage on our honeymoon!'

'Honeymoon?' Jo stared up at him in astonishment. 'Is that necessary?'

'No. But it's customary. For obvious reasons I'd rather our marriage presented itself as the normal kind to the world at large.' Rufus held her by the shoulders. 'Look on a honeymoon as a therapeutic exercise—a means to get used to being married before we actually set up house together. Any preferences?'

Jo thought it over. 'I'd rather not fly anywhere. I get a bit sick in a plane. It might not be good for the baby.' Her chin lifted. 'And I'd rather not go anywhere you went with Claire, either.'

'I wouldn't be oaf enough to suggest it,' he said tersely. 'Give me credit for some sensitivity.'

Suddenly there was hostility in the air. Jo turned away, but Rufus caught her by the shoulders and turned her back to face him.

'Sorry,' he said shortly. 'Just tell me where you'd like to go and I'll make the necessary arrangements. Think about it for a day or two if you like.'

She nodded silently, and he bent suddenly and kissed her cheek.

'Meet me in town tomorrow for lunch, Jo.'

'But I want to work—'

'Just this once. We need to go shopping. For a ring,' he added.

Her eyes glittered with dismay. 'Rufus, I don't *want* a ring!'

'Possibly not,' he said wearily. 'Nevertheless you're going to have one.'

Jo stared at him mutinously, then sighed. 'Oh, very well.'

'I'll meet you outside the lawcourts at twelve. The ring first, then we'll have lunch, and after that I'll leave you in peace for a day or two. If that's what you want.' He waited, almost as though he expected her to contradict him. When she didn't Rufus turned abruptly and went to the door. 'Goodnight, Jo.'

'Goodnight,' she said, so forlornly that he came back to her, took her in his arms and kissed her swiftly on the mouth.

'Goodnight again, Jocasta Fielding. Sleep well.'

Then Rufus was gone, and Jo, more comforted by his kiss than she would have liked him to know, went to the telephone to ask her mother's advice on what to wear for Rory Grierson's wedding and to give answers to all the questions Rose Fielding hadn't been able to ask in front of Rufus.

Later, in bed, Jo came to the conclusion that things could be a lot worse. Rufus had met with her mother's unqualified approval, the green dress, with the purchase of a smart hat, was deemed perfectly suitable for Rory Grierson's wedding, and, all things considered, decided Jo, marrying Rufus was a prospect which grew dangerously more attractive by the minute.

If only... She clamped down on her thoughts savagely. It was pointless to wish for the moon. She knew perfectly well that Rufus was marrying her purely for the baby's sake. While she was marrying him for the simple reason that she loved him more and more each day. Baby or no baby.

CHAPTER SIX

By THE time Jo arrived in town to meet Rufus next day he was pacing up and down, glancing at his watch. His face cleared as she dashed up to him.

'Hey, slow down! Where've you been?'

'I was working and forgot the time,' she said breathlessly. 'I had to rush to make myself presentable.'

'You look good, Jo—positively blooming.' Rufus took her by the elbow to walk through the gardens towards the shops in Broad Street. 'I've already been to Fournier's. They've got a selection of rings ready for you.'

'I don't want anything too showy,' she warned. 'A ring of any kind makes me feel—well, fraudulent.'

Rufus stopped near the central fountain, and took her by the hands. 'Jo, this is for real. All of it.' He smiled down into her troubled eyes. 'Don't look like that. In time you might even like being married to me.'

She smiled. 'Stranger things have happened, I suppose. It's just that everything's such a rush.'

'Once we're married you can relax,' he promised. 'Now let's go shopping. And, just in case you were wondering, Claire's ring came from a London jeweller.'

Grateful for his perception, Jo entered into the spirit of the purchase with more enthusiasm, and half an hour later her small brown hand wore an antique gold ring set with green tourmalines interspersed with diamonds.

'You should have had the emerald,' said Rufus as he hurried her from the shop.

'I preferred this one,' said Jo, admiring it, then realised they were crossing the road towards his car. 'Where are we going for lunch?'

'To my parents' house,' he said, thrusting her in the passenger seat.

'But—'

'No buts, Jo. I knew you'd argue if I told you sooner. Mother wanted to make it a celebration dinner tonight, but I'm due in London later this afternoon, and I'll be away for most of the week, so lunch it is.'

Afterwards Jo was glad she'd had no time to be nervous, since both Griersons were kindness itself to her over lunch at their comfortable, conventional house on the outskirts of Pennington. They gave Jo a warm welcome, and made it clear they thought their son's choice of a second wife the most natural thing in the world. They mentioned Claire without constraint, and complimented a guilty Jo on her sensitivity in refusing to announce the engagement sooner in deference to Claire's memory. After only a short discussion of wedding plans Rufus rushed Jo away again soon after the meal. He gave his departure for London as an excuse, and promised his mother they'd linger as long as she liked on their next visit.

'I won't come in,' said Rufus, when he drew up in Bruton Road. 'I would have postponed this London trip if I could, but with the honeymoon coming up I thought I'd better get it over with. Come to a decision yet?'

Jo nodded. Because their honeymoon wouldn't be the normal arrangement of two people wanting to spend as much time alone together as possible, she'd had a brainwave in the night. 'I'd like a plush London hotel for a long weekend, with trips to theatres and art galleries and so on. The family holiday was usually a cottage near a Welsh beach, and otherwise I had just the one holiday with Claire and her family in France. The bright lights rather appeal.'

'Done,' he said promptly. 'I'll organise it while I'm up there. Any particular plush hotel?'

She shook her head, smiling. 'You choose.'

'What an amenable little wife you're going to be!'

'Don't count on it!'

Rufus reached out to flip a finger across her cheek. 'Take care while I'm gone. By which I mean eat something at intervals while you're glued to your computer.'

'I won't be. Mother's coming for a day or two tomorrow. More shopping,' said Jo, resigned.

Rufus felt in his pockets and produced a key. 'In that case why not take her to Beaufort Crescent and show her over the house?'

Jo beamed at him. 'Why, thank you; she'd love that.' She hesitated. 'Rufus, thank you for the ring. It's beautiful.'

'Which reminds me.' He looked at her in silence for a moment. 'Don't take this the wrong way, Jocasta Fielding, but this shopping of yours—does it involve a wedding dress of some kind?'

'Of course it does. Why?'

'Since it's my fault you need one, would you let me foot the bill?'

Jo stiffened. 'Absolutely not.'

Rufus reached out a detaining hand as she turned to get out of the car. 'My offer was well intentioned, I swear. Take heart. I'm a quick learner. I never make the same mistake twice.'

Jo's eyes took on a feline glitter as she gave him a smile as sweet and cold as a sorbet. 'I'll take good care to see you don't.'

His answering smile was tigerish. 'If you're referring to my hopes about the exact nature of our future relationship, as I always say, Jo—never refuse a request before it's made.'

Jo's eyes flashed dangerously, and without another word she got out of the car and hurried up the path to the house, grinding her teeth in fury as Rufus drove away before she even reached the door.

Surprisingly, the biting little exchange had no effect on her creativity. Jo spent the rest of the day in front of her computer, elated to find that she was only days away from finishing the first rough draft of her novel. Later that evening, when protesting muscles forced her to stop at last, Jo was on her way to a hot bath when the telephone rang.

'Jo?' said Rufus.

'Yes.'

'Are you still angry with me?'

'Of course not,' she said airily. 'I never gave it another thought.'

'I'll make a note not to offer you money again.'

'And I promise not to keep reminding you that this marriage is purely an agreement on paper,' she countered.

There was silence for a moment. 'So now that's all cleared up,' he went on at last, 'did you manage to get some writing done this afternoon?'

'I certainly did. I got on like a house on fire. I worked late to make up for my day off tomorrow when Mother's here.'

'Give her my regards, Jo.'

'I will. She's going to help me choose a hat for your brother's wedding.'

'Don't get too tired.'

'I won't. In any case I think the swollen-ankles bit happens later on, not at this stage.'

'Still no morning sickness?'

'No. In fact,' added Jo, 'I don't feel pregnant at all yet. Perhaps I'm not, and all your arrangements are unnecessary after all.'

'I'm sure you'll inform me if that's the case.'

'Of course. Not much point in getting married if there's no baby,' she said acidly.

'Quite so,' agreed Rufus at his driest. 'I'll ring you when I get back, Jo. Goodnight.'

Rose Fielding stayed only one night with Jo, sympathetic with her daughter's eagerness to get on with the novel while it was going so well. Their shopping spree was very successful. Mrs Fielding bought Jo a dress in pale, muted pink, bias-cut from pure silk crêpe, and flatly refused to let her daughter see the price tag. She insisted Jo splurge her own money on the hat, a wide-brimmed natural straw with a cluster of pink silk roses rioting over the brim. Jo couldn't resist the extravagant confection, despite the price, but chose a plain straw boater with green ribbons to wear to Rory's wedding.

'Pity I couldn't have worn the same hat to both,' she complained as she settled the bill.

'No, Jocasta Fielding, definitely not!' Mrs Fielding chuckled. 'I can just see Thalia's face if you did that.'

'No doubt the heavenly twins are turning up in designer gear from head to toe?' asked Jo as, feeling very pleased with themselves, they ate lunch together in the department store's restaurant.

'Probably. They were both wild with excitement at the news, though I fancy Thalia thought senility had finally overtaken me when I said you were marrying Rufus.' Rose looked at her daughter searchingly. 'Darling, that's an exquisite ring, and Rufus made all the right noises the day you came to lunch, but would you *be* marrying him if you weren't pregnant?'

Jo made no attempt to lie. 'No, I wouldn't. But he's always wanted a family, which is why Claire went through hoops to try and provide him with one. For my part I would have done without a husband, but Rufus wants his child to grow up in the same house as both parents. It's a great house, Mother; we'll go and see it when we've finished here.'

'Was the house a deciding factor, then?' asked her mother in amusement.

'It helped. So in three weeks, much to my astonishment, I'm marrying Claire's husband. A bit hard to believe at times.'

Rose coughed delicately. 'If it's so hard to believe, how did you come to get pregnant in the first place?'

Jo flushed. 'In the usual way.' Not even to her mother could she confess that she'd been hopelessly in love with Rufus all along.

Jo had dreaded Rory Grierson's wedding service, and relaxed only when it was over.

She released her grip on Rufus' hand as the wedding party moved down the aisle, and smiled at him in reassurance when he bent to peer under the brim of her boater.

'All right?' he said in an undertone, and she nodded.

'Yes. Though I'm glad we're having a civil ceremony, not all this.'

'I did wonder if you minded about that,' he said in her ear as they followed the others out of the church. 'We could just as easily be married in church.'

'No! I'd much rather not.' Jo shivered despite the sunshine as they merged into the crowd. It had been a poignant moment when Rory and his Susannah promised to love and cherish each other until death parted them. It had parted Claire from Rufus with such indecent haste.

The reception was in a large marquee in the garden of the bride's family, and Jo was congratulated by several people anxious to express their pleasure over the fact that Rufus was about to marry again. But the day was by no means the ordeal Jo had expected. Claire's wedding breakfast had been in the ballroom of a London hotel, very formal and correct, with a master of ceremonies and a string quartet, whereas Susannah's was an informal family party, with children running everywhere, and once the speeches were over the bride and groom circulated among their guests, spending time at every table.

When they paused to talk to Rufus and Jo, both Rory and his radiant, euphoric Susannah made it gratifyingly plain that they were glad she was marrying Rufus.

'He's had a rough year, and yours must have been pretty much the same, Jo,' said Rory, who was a younger, stockier version of his brother. 'I couldn't have been more pleased when I heard you two had got together. Welcome to the family.'

It was impossible not to respond to the couple's warm sincerity, and Jo smiled and thanked them for their good wishes.

'Once Rory and Susannah leave we can do the same,' Rufus said as the couple moved on to the next group of guests. 'How are you coping?'

'Quite well. I rather dreaded meeting so many of your family.'

'Why?'

'Because the last time I met them was at *your* wedding,' she reminded him. 'No one mentioned that, of course, but I could tell it struck most people the moment they laid eyes on me.'

'You're not the type people forget, Jo. I like the hat, by the way.'

'Thank you.' She smiled up at him. 'Would you believe I had to buy *two* hats? Mother wouldn't let me wear the same one to both weddings.'

Rufus grinned. 'Such a passion for economy augurs well for your housekeeping.'

Jo chuckled. 'Wait to experience it before you get too excited.'

His eyes met hers with meaning. 'It would be an unnatural man who didn't get excited at the prospect of marrying *you*, Jocasta.'

'What on earth are you saying to make the poor girl blush like that?' demanded Mrs Grierson. 'Come on, you two. Rory and Susannah are just off. I've brought you some confetti, Jo.'

Once all the rice and confetti had been thrown at the protesting pair, and the car had moved off down the road, trailing old boots and silver balloons, Rufus took Jo to say her goodbyes to the bride's parents, then paused for a few minutes' conversation with his father while Mrs Grierson took Jo aside and asked if there was anything she could do to help with the next wedding arrangements.

Jo thanked her future mother-in-law warmly, told her everything was in hand, then passed on an invitation to lunch at Willowdene Lodge to meet Rose Fielding.

Mrs Grierson gave her a delighted little hug. 'How lovely. Thank your mother very much, my dear. I look forward to meeting her again.'

In the house in Beaufort Crescent later, with a striped butcher's apron over her green dress, Jo cooked the promised chicken *cacciatora* for Rufus, who came down to offer his help once he'd changed his wedding formality for a cotton sweater and jeans.

'Just talk to me while I cook,' she said, pounding garlic and rosemary together while chicken breasts browned in a skillet.

'I should have taken you out for a meal, not let you slave over a hot stove after all the nervous strain today,' said Rufus as he laid the table.

'I much prefer an evening in.' Jo added some wine vinegar to the pan, then dodged away as it hissed. 'I'm glad I went to the wedding. It was a very relaxed, happy occasion—once the church service was over, anyway.'

'I saw you flinch at the "death us do part" bit,' he said quietly. 'At least you won't be required to say that.'

'Good.' Jo sprinkled herbs and garlic over the chicken, seasoned it, and asked Rufus for a glass of the wine he was opening.

'Thirsty?'

'No. It's to go in the chicken. Then I put a lid on it and leave it for half an hour while I make a green salad.'

Rufus breathed in the aroma with pleasure. 'I thought you were a no-nonsense cook, Jo.'

'I am. My repertoire is very limited, I promise you.' She stood back as the wine sizzled in the pan, waited for a while to let the alcohol burn off, then turned the heat down low and put the lid on. 'Perhaps you'd better buy me a cookery book for a wedding present.'

'I've already bought you a wedding present,' he informed her.

Jo turned sharply, her eyes wide with consternation. 'I was joking! I don't need a present, Rufus.'

'I know that. You're a very undemanding bride. But I think you'll like this one. We can go upstairs and inspect it after dinner.'

Wondering what she could present Rufus with in return, Jo put a salad together, made a dressing for it, then cut bread and took butter from the fridge. Rufus put them on the table, then lit the candles he'd set out earlier.

'Nice touch,' said Jo, and smiled at him. 'Adds a festive note to my no-nonsense menu.'

Rufus ate the meal with such flattering relish that Jo relaxed and enjoyed it herself as they discussed the events of the day.

'Right,' said Rufus, when his brand-new dishwasher was switched on. 'Come upstairs and tell me if I made the right choice of present.'

'Couldn't you bring it down?' she asked as they went up the curving staircase together.

'Not without risk to my person,' he assured her with a grin, and showed her into the smaller of the two main bedrooms with a flourish.

The room was bare except for a small, beautiful desk under the window, complete with laptop computer. Jo gave an exclamation, and looked up at Rufus in delight. 'Both of them for me? Rufus, what a wonderful present!'

'Eighteenth-century elegance allied to twentieth-century technology,' he said, with a flourish. 'The rest of the furnishings I leave to you, of course. But I thought if inspiration struck when you weren't in the mood for transferring to Bruton Road you could jot notes down here.'

'Thank you *so* much, Rufus.' Jo decided against kissing him, and gave him a radiant smile instead. 'It's the best present I've ever had. I just love the desk.'

She pulled out drawers reverently, then opened the computer like a child with a new toy. After a moment or two she closed it again. 'No,' she said firmly. 'If I start playing with that I'll never stop. I'll wait until I move in.'

'Talking of which,' said Rufus as they went downstairs again, 'I'm afraid you'll have to take a day off again on Monday to choose your bedroom furniture. Meet me for lunch again?'

Jo nodded. 'I'll work longer tomorrow instead.'

Rufus frowned. 'I thought you never worked on weekends.'

'I don't normally, but if I do the last two thousand words or so tomorrow I've finished.'

'A good thing I refused, then, when Mother asked us to Sunday lunch. I thought you might have had enough of my family for a while, so I refused—very gracefully, of course—on your behalf.'

'Oh, did you?' she said belligerently.

'Which is just as well,' he said smoothly, 'since you're bent on labouring all day tomorrow instead.'

The wind taken out of her sails, Jo couldn't let fly with the angry protest she'd been about to make, and Rufus, lips twitching, suggested he come round late the next evening instead, to make sure she didn't write all day.

'I'd rather my bride had circles under her eyes after the honeymoon than on her wedding day,' he said, smiling at the wave of scarlet which rose behind Jo's rapidly fading tan.

She gave him a hostile glare and marched into the small, elegant drawing room to collect her hat. 'In that case, rather than let you down on the day I'd better go home and get some beauty sleep.' Not that any amount of beauty sleep would transform her into a bride as dazzling as Claire.

Rufus caught her by the shoulders and turned her round. 'I was joking,' he said roughly. 'I'm worried about your health, Jocasta Fielding, not your appearance. I'll come round about eight tomorrow night—and I'll expect to find that blasted computer of yours turned off when I do.'

She stared at him mutinously for a moment, then shrugged. 'Oh, very well. Though you did promise you wouldn't fuss.'

'This has nothing to do with the baby,' he said with emphasis, his eyes boring into hers. 'When I came back from London on Thursday you looked like a ghost. I was worried.'

Jo's eyes fell. 'You needn't worry about *me*,' she muttered. 'I can look after myself.'

'Perhaps you'd furnish me with proof of that statement,' he said sardonically, 'by doing a rather better job of it from now on.'

She smiled sheepishly. 'It's only because I'm so near the end, Rufus—like a racehorse in sight of the finishing post.'

'And what happens once you've finished the novel? Will you suffer from anticlimax?'

'Possibly.' She eyed him narrowly. 'You've never asked me what the book is about, Rufus. Does that mean you're not interested?'

'Hell, no—quite the reverse.' He gave her a crooked grin. 'But our relationship is beset with rather more pitfalls than the normal kind, Jo. With you I proceed with care, afraid of trespass.'

'How very cautious!'

He raised an eyebrow. 'Wary, rather than cautious.'

'It's a rites-of-passage theme, about two girls growing up, their lives taking different directions, and what happens to them as adults.' She nodded in answer to the involuntary question in his eyes. 'Yes, there's a lot of Claire and me in it. At least to begin with. But after a while the girls took on personalities and characters of their own, and the story develops very differently. They both fall in love with the same man.'

'Definitely fiction,' he said drily.

Jo laughed, and detached herself. 'And now I must go home and get to bed. Weddings are tiring.'

'I hope you won't find ours too exhausting.'

'With only a handful of us to celebrate, I doubt it.' Jo smiled at him as they went outside to the car. 'Thank you again for the present, Rufus. I'll do my best to think of something equally inspired for you.'

Rufus halted halfway down the steps to the pavement. 'I don't need a present from you, Jo. That wasn't the object of the exercise at all.'

'I know,' she said calmly, and patted his arm. 'But it seems only fair you should have something to mark the occasion.'

'I doubt that I'll find it easy to forget, gift or no gift,' he assured her, and she giggled as they drove off.

'No, I don't suppose you will. Especially if the bride turns pea-green with morning sickness during the ceremony!'

'Are you likely to do that?' Rufus inquired with interest.

'No—I was only joking. I feel very well, actually.' She shot a look at his profile. 'Would you prefer it if I did?'

'What kind of a man do you think I am?' he demanded irritably. 'Of course I wouldn't.'

'I merely meant,' said Jo patiently, 'that you might see it as confirmation of my condition. Because I don't seem to be suffering from any of the usual symptoms.'

Rufus stopped the car in Bruton Road and turned to her. 'Are you hoping against hope that maybe there was a mistake?'

Jo sighed. 'If I'm honest . . .'

'And you invariably are!'

She shrugged. 'I suppose I'd rather not *be* pregnant, but since I am I promise to make the best of it. Not that I know much about babies.'

'Neither do I. We'll learn together.' He leaned across and kissed her cheek. 'Goodnight, Jo. I won't come in. Have an early night.'

'Do you want me to cook for you tomorrow night?'

Rufus shook his head, giving her a smug smile. 'No, thanks. I may have refused the lunch invitation on your behalf, but *I* shall be wolfing down Mother's roast beef and Yorkshire pudding as usual, believe me!'

'Pig,' said Jo wrathfully. 'I think I've changed my mind about marrying you after all.'

Rufus looked at her, suddenly very sober. 'Have you, Jo?'

Her eyes fell. 'No. No, of course not. As I told you before, once I make a promise, I keep it.'

CHAPTER SEVEN

THE following week went by rapidly. Jo finished the first draft of her book in triumph and in the ensuing haze of euphoria made only half-hearted noises about extravagance when Rufus insisted on an antique brass bed for her room rather than the modern, far less expensive piece of furniture she'd expected. The bed was wide and handsome, its only flaw from Jo's point of view the fact that she would sleep in it alone, instead of in her husband's arms every night, like any other self-respecting bride.

Jo described it with sparkling eyes during the family lunch that Sunday, her mother laughing when Rufus said he'd expected warfare at the shop over the price.

'Your daughter possesses an over-developed streak of economy, Rose,' he told his future mother-in-law.

'I'm afraid her upbringing is to blame for that,' she said ruefully.

'You should be thanking your lucky stars for it, Rufus,' said his mother.

George Grierson winked at Jo. 'Best not to economise over the nuptial couch, my dear!'

The lunch party was a great success, and afterwards Rufus left his parents chatting with Rose Fielding over coffee while he took Jo for a walk before driving his parents home.

'I thought it best to stay with Mother this last week. I knew she wouldn't suggest it herself,' Jo added as they strolled through the parkland surrounding

Willowdene Manor, 'but she was very pleased when I did.'

'Only a week to go,' said Rufus, taking her hand. 'Any regrets?'

Jo stopped and looked up at him very squarely. 'Qualms rather than regrets. How about you?'

He shook his head. 'I think we'll do very well together.'

'And baby makes three,' said Jo pensively. 'I still can't quite believe that bit.'

'Neither can I,' said Rufus gravely, then smiled. 'But no doubt our offspring will make his—or her—presence felt soon enough. Too soon for you, probably.'

Jo nodded philosophically, and waved at the west wing of Willowdene Manor as they approached it. 'That's Thalia's bit. You'll like her husband, Charlie. They don't get back from their holiday in Italy until Tuesday. She'll be furious she missed lunch today. If she'd been home she'd have tried bullying Mother into having it at her place.'

'Your mother doesn't strike me **as** the type to give in to bullying.'

'She isn't—which doesn't stop Thalia from trying.' Jo giggled. 'She was mad as fire because I didn't invite her along to choose the dress.'

'Will I like it?' asked Rufus.

'I hope so—I don't know.' Jo bit her lip in sudden anxiety. 'There's so much I don't know about you, Rufus.'

'Nor I about you,' he agreed, unmoved. 'We'll learn as we go along.'

'You make it sound like the easiest thing in the world!'

Rufus stopped under the shedding leaves of a beech tree. 'Then I'm wrong. Marriage isn't easy—both partners need to work at it to make it a success.'

'But you've been married before,' Jo said bluntly. 'I'm a novice.'

He looked down at her, his face giving no clue to his thoughts. 'Will you take umbrage, Jocasta Fielding, if I say that my first marriage is unlikely to be of help with my second?'

She looked away. 'I realise that. Claire was the perfect wife. And you were in love with her,' she added quietly.

'Actually I didn't mean that at all. I meant that you are as unlike Claire as it's possible to be, so marriage with you will be correspondingly different.'

'Claire was happy just to be your wife,' said Jo morosely. 'I'm not like that, Rufus. I'm just not the type to revel in lunchtime drinks parties and having people to dinner. She adored all that.'

'Don't worry.' Rufus smiled. 'When we entertain I'll get someone in to cater.'

'You don't trust my cooking, then!'

'As a matter of fact, I do. But if you're coping with a baby and a deadline simultaneously I won't expect you to produce a cordon bleu meal as well.'

'Good! I'm relieved.' Jo's eyes darkened. 'Your friends are bound to make comparisons.'

'We entertained Claire's hunt crowd far more than my own particular friends,' he said, shrugging. '"To be honest"—I quote—I would have been quite happy to eat a scratch meal in the kitchen now and then, or eat supper off a tray sometimes in front of the television. It was Claire who insisted on candles and flowers in the dining room every night.'

'I suppose it was the way she was brought up,' said Jo sadly. '*I* wasn't.'

'That needn't worry you either. Do whatever *you* want, Jo. And forget the entertaining. I suggest we get used to entertaining each other for a while first.'

'That worries me even more,' she said candidly.

'You're afraid I'll bore you?'

'No, that I'll bore *you*.'

'Would you care if you did?' he asked with interest.

'I'd care if I bored anyone,' she retorted, indignant as she saw his eyes were dancing. 'It may be a joke to you, Rufus Grierson—'

'Of course it's a joke,' he said forcefully, and caught her by the elbows. 'If we run out of conversation you can read me extracts from your book, and I'll regale you with witty legal anecdotes. As a last resort we'll watch television. And after the baby comes we won't have time to bore each other. We'll be taking turns to entertain our offspring when he cries all evening.'

'She,' contradicted Jo, laughing, as they resumed their walk. 'By the way, are you wearing a morning coat on the day, Rufus?'

He paused as they reached the Lodge gate, his eyes narrowed. 'Would you rather I didn't?'

Jo smiled diffidently. 'Couldn't you just wear one of your ordinary suits? Not that any of your suits look ordinary, precisely, but you know what I mean.'

'I know exactly, Jo,' he said quietly. 'You'd rather your wedding was as different as possible from Claire's.'

'Yes.' Her eyes met his squarely. 'Does that sound petty?'

'No. I'm in full agreement. I'll spread the word.'

'Thank you, Rufus.'

Rose Fielding appeared at the Lodge door, and beckoned them in. 'Come on, you two, I've made tea.'

When Jocasta Grierson was shown into the hotel suite that Rufus had reserved for their honeymoon she was too tired to feel the awkwardness she had been convinced would be inevitable once they were alone together as man and wife. But she was impressed, she admitted secretly as Rufus tipped the porter. The rooms were furnished with the essence of luxurious comfort, the windows overlooked Hyde Park in all its autumnal glory, and for the crowning touch Rufus had ordered champagne and flowers to make the occasion as special as he possibly could for her.

'They wanted to throw in chocolates as well, but I declined,' he said, smiling as Jo explored.

'Wise move,' she agreed, yawning. 'Thank you very much for the rest. It's all quite wonderful—and frighteningly expensive too, I imagine.'

'It's only for four nights,' he reminded her. 'You jibbed at a longer stay.'

She bounced gently on one of the large beds. 'The city lights would pall if we stayed longer.' She smiled up at him. 'I'm definitely a small-town girl.'

'Then why choose London for the honeymoon?' he demanded, loosening his tie.

'Because in our particular circumstances London, and all it has to offer, seemed the most sensible choice.'

'You mean that theatres and museums might prevent me from hankering after the delights normal bridegrooms expect,' said Rufus suavely.

Jo glared at him. 'Since you mention it, yes,' she snapped, and opened her case to unpack.

Rufus came to her swiftly and turned her to face him. 'Pax, Jo. I was teasing. When I made the reservation I stipulated two beds, remember. But if you're that nervous I can sleep on the sofa in the other room.'

Which was so far from what she really wanted that her lashes came down like a screen to hide her eyes. 'Of course not,' she said stiffly. 'It's just that it's been a lovely day after all, Rufus—'

'After all?' he said quickly.

She nodded. 'I didn't expect it to be so relaxed, I suppose. Because of Claire. But the ceremony was so quick and simple, and the lunch afterwards was such fun, I enjoyed it all far more than I'd dared hope. So don't spoil it for me now, Rufus.'

He touched a finger to her cheek. 'I'm sorry, Jo. Look, leave the unpacking for a while—let's have some champagne.'

Jo smiled at him hopefully. 'I'd rather have some tea.'

'Then tea you shall have, Mrs Grierson,' he said promptly, and went over to the phone to call Room Service.

From then on Rufus set out deliberately to be the perfect companion, beginning that evening with dinner in the hotel's famous dining room. They ate late, giving Jo the respite of a long, leisurely bath beforehand and a rest on one of the beds while Rufus watched satellite television in the other room. She slept for a while, and when she woke Rufus was dressed, ready for dinner, a drink beside him as he read the evening paper.

Jo slid off the bed in a hurry. 'Sorry, Rufus—shan't be long.'

He looked up from the paper with a smile. 'Take as long as you like. You look better.'

'I feel better. I seem to need more sleep these days.'

When Jo was bathed and made up and looking, even to her own eyes, rather stunning in her wedding dress, she rejoined Rufus and handed him a box. 'Your wedding present.' She watched in trepidation as he opened it and drew out a gold half-hunter watch with a chain ending in a quartz and crystal fob.

He stared at it, utterly taken aback. 'Good Lord— Jo, I don't know what to say.'

Jo bit her lip. 'Don't you like it?'

Rufus smiled at her with a warmth he rarely displayed. 'How could I not? It's magnificent!'

'The provenance is in the box,' said Jo breathlessly. 'The watch dates from about 1900 and the chain a little later.'

Rufus stripped off his wrist-watch and threaded the new chain through the buttonhole in his lapel, then inserted the watch very carefully into his top pocket. He laid the box on a table, then bent and kissed her very deliberately on the mouth. 'Thank you very much indeed, Jo. A special kiss for a very special present. I'll treasure it—keep it to hand on to our son.' He slid a hand down and patted her stomach.

'Or daughter,' she said firmly, and he laughed.

'Whichever.'

The days passed quickly in visits to the British Museum and the National Gallery, to Westminster Abbey and St Paul's Cathedral. They walked in Hyde Park and did some shopping in Bond Street, saw a hit musical and a straight play, and afterwards dined late at the hotel. Jo went to bed each night too tired to lie awake longing in vain for her husband to make love to her.

The last night before their return to Pennington, Jo refused another trip to the theatre, preferring an earlier dinner and a film afterwards on the satellite television in their suite.

'Whatever you say,' yawned Rufus, professing himself only too pleased with the arrangement. 'In fact you can have dinner up here if you like.'

Jo liked the idea a lot. 'My feet are hurting after all that shopping,' she confessed.

'Then take a long, hot bath, get into your dressing gown and we'll choose something special for our last evening.' Rufus smiled at her lazily. 'Are you sorry to be heading back to life in Pennington?'

'No, not a bit!' Jo slumped on the sofa beside him to watch the television news. 'I've got the draft of my novel to work on, remember.'

'I've been thinking about that,' said Rufus, eyeing her. 'I know we agreed you'd use your flat for your writing, but for the time being could you work on your draft at home?'

Home, thought Jo. 'Why, Rufus?'

'We're expecting a few deliveries in the next couple of weeks—furniture and so on. It would be easier if you were on hand when they arrive.'

She eyed him curiously. 'What did you do before?'

'Suffered a great deal of inconvenience.' Rufus shrugged. 'But if you feel you can't work there—'

'I can work anywhere,' she assured him. 'The muse deserts me over mental pressure, not change of location. But you'll have to fetch my word processor from Bruton Road.'

'Done,' he said promptly. 'Shall I shower first or do you want your usual wallow now?'

'You go first,' she said absently, then smiled up at him, surprising an odd look in the ink-dark eyes which so rarely betrayed his feelings. 'What's the matter?'

'Nothing,' he said expressionlessly. 'Nothing at all.'

The evening was a pleasant change from the frantic activity of the days preceding it. They ate lobster salad, followed by *tarte tatin*, and Rufus finally opened the bottle of champagne that Jo had refused on their first day in preference to tea.

Curled up on the sofa, relaxed with good food, Jo accepted a glass of the pale, bubbling wine, and Rufus sat beside her to watch the film, which was a light romantic comedy perfectly in tune with her mood.

'Though I usually prefer dark, atmospheric thrillers,' she told him as the opening credits rolled. 'I love going to the cinema. But this is the next best thing.'

'I haven't been to the cinema in years,' he remarked. 'I'll take you to the Regal when we get back, if you like.'

Jo nodded enthusiastically. 'Yes, please!'

Silence fell between them as they watched the film, which was light and unusually witty but towards the end leaned towards bedroom scenes rather more than Jo would have liked. She sipped at her champagne, growing tenser by the minute, wishing she had the strength of mind to suggest they watched something less erotic. It was a great relief when the film was over at last.

'Not bad,' commented Rufus, and refilled her glass.

'The fairy-tale ending was a bit contrived, I thought,' said Jo casually.

'Good for box office, I suppose. People like fairy-tale endings.' Rufus stared down into his glass. 'They don't happen often enough in real life.'

How true, thought Jo forlornly. She got to her feet, and to her dismay found she wasn't in entire control of them. 'I think I'll go to bed.'

Rufus got up, his eyes gleaming with amusement. 'Are you by any chance unsteady on your pins, Mrs Grierson?'

'Yes,' she said sheepishly. 'I think I am.'

'You were so hot under the collar over the love scenes you drank two glasses of champagne,' he said, grinning.

'Did I? *Two?*' She giggled. 'In that case you'd better give me a hand to the bathroom.'

Rufus complied, laughing as he guided her weaving feet across the room. 'Can you manage?'

'I hope so!'

When she emerged from the bathroom some time later Rufus was waiting outside the door for her. 'All right?' he asked.

'Perfectly.' She eyed the distance to the bed doubtfully, and Rufus chuckled and picked her up.

'Allow me!' He carried her to the bed, laying her down on it with exaggerated care. 'A good thing you didn't dress for dinner tonight.'

'It's only my legs which let me down,' she assured him, settling back against the pillows. 'The rest of me seems much the same as usual.'

Rufus sat on the edge of the bed, smiling at her. 'So how are you, Jocasta Grierson? The honeymoon's almost over and you've survived very well from where I'm sitting. Do you agree? Or have you been pining for your attic all along?'

'No,' she assured him. 'I've enjoyed it all immensely. It's my first experience of a hotel like this.'

'It won't be your last, Jo,' he promised softly, and leaned over her, a hand either side of her on the bed.

Jo gazed up into his face, fascinated as she saw the pupils of his eyes widen to engulf the dark iris. They lay there motionless, eyes locked as Rufus hung over her, balanced on his hands, then suddenly his eyelids came down like shutters and he stretched out beside her, burying his face in her hair as he took her in his arms.

'I so badly want to hold you like this,' he said, his voice muffled against her hair. 'I really thought I could do it, you know.'

'Do what?' she whispered, her heart beating thickly.

'Share a room with you and keep my distance.' He raised his head suddenly to look down into her heavy eyes. 'Can you believe that I just want to sleep with you, Jo?'

To her infinite regret Jo knew that Rufus meant what he said. There was no hint of sexual persuasion in his embrace. She sighed. 'Get in, then.'

He stared at her in disbelief. 'You mean that?'

'Yes.'

'If I turn out all the lights and do the usual night-time things in the bathroom, will you have changed your mind by the time I come back?' he demanded.

'No.' She smiled at him. 'But if you don't hurry it up I'll be asleep.'

Within a remarkably short time Rufus slid into bed beside her, teeth brushed, newly shaved, clad in the pyjama trousers worn, she suspected, out of deference to his new room-mate.

'Do you always wear pyjamas?' she asked as he stretched out beside her with a sigh.

'No. I bought three new pairs just for the occasion. Tonight I'm wearing tasteful navy blue.'

She giggled. 'And I'm in tasteful pink—suitable for a blushing bride.'

'You're just the slightest bit stoned, aren't you?' he said, amused. 'For which I'm very grateful.'

'Why?' she asked, yawning.

'If you weren't I'd hardly be here in your bed, would I?'

In no mood for debate Jo burrowed deep into the pillow with a sigh, her heart giving a sudden thump when an arm encircled her waist and drew her close. For a moment she lay tense, then relaxed, and, instead of lying awake as she fully expected, fell asleep very quickly in the warmth of her husband's embrace.

Jo woke in the night to visit the bathroom, and afterwards, half-asleep, slid back into the warm bed, straight into arms outstretched in welcome to receive her. Instantly Jo found herself wide awake, aware in every fibre of the hard male body against her own. Her pulse quickened and she raised her head to find her mouth only a hair's breadth from her husband's.

Rufus breathed in sharply, then lowered his head until their lips met. He kissed her mouth, her eyelids, returning to her mouth in between attention to her cheekbones and her earlobes, his hands moving over her in caresses so subtle and cajoling that she felt as though her bones were melting.

She knew he was holding himself on a tight rein while he sought to undermine her non-existent defences, but their kisses quickly grew wilder, their breathing ragged, until Jo could no longer control little choked sounds of response as his caressing fingers touched off sparks of flame which ran along her veins and set her body on fire. He hung over her, his eyes glittering down into hers with a question she answered with an involuntary thrust of her hips against his aroused body, and with a smothered sound he took possession of her with a fiery tenderness, making love to her gently at first, then not gently at all as the rhythm of their loving became faster and fiercer until fulfilment overwhelmed them simultaneously, teaching them that their first time together had been no fluke of never-to-be repeated rapture.

Jo woke to daylight, and muted voices in the other room, and sat up groggily, her face hot as the events of the night came rushing back.

'Good morning,' said Rufus, strolling into the bedroom, wearing his dressing gown. 'Breakfast is served. I wish I'd asked for it later—you could have slept on for a while.'

'Good morning,' muttered Jo, clutching the covers to her chest. 'What time is it?'

'Eight-thirty.' Rufus sat on the edge of the bed and detached one of her hands, holding it in his as he looked at her. 'Are you all right, Jo?'

Unwillingly she met his eyes. 'Yes, Rufus. A bit embarrassed, but I'm fine.'

His face relaxed a little. 'Honest, as always. I wondered if the champagne had something to do with your lack of resistance in the night.'

Surely he knew why she'd responded so joyously? 'Thank you for providing excuses,' she said drily. 'But that had worn off by three in the morning, Rufus. What's the matter?' she added. 'You look worried.'

'It didn't strike me until I woke up this morning—with you in my arms, incidentally—that I forgot about the baby.'

Jo sat suddenly motionless, her face drained of expression. 'Ah, yes, the baby. The reason why we are here in this extraordinary situation in the first place.' She shrugged. 'All seems to be well, I think.' Her eyes glittered coldly to cover her hurt. 'But since you're so concerned for the safety of your child I suggest we keep firmly to our own beds in future.'

She slid out of bed, ignored the nightgown on the floor, and made for the bathroom without haste, well aware that her husband's eyes were riveted to her nude, slender back until she closed the door behind her.

CHAPTER EIGHT

TRAFFIC was too heavy for much conversation on the journey out of London, for which Jo was profoundly grateful. All through breakfast she'd kept up a steady flow of small talk over the morning papers, and Rufus, after one or two firmly rebuffed attempts to turn the conversation to more personal matters, responded with cool courtesy, other than remonstrating with her for eating nothing. With a bright smile she blamed a slight hangover for her lack of appetite, told him never to mention lobster and champagne in her hearing again, and went off to pack.

Jo felt so miserable as they headed down the motorway that she apologised politely for her poor company, and announced she'd try and doze a little. After which Rufus drove in complete silence until they were on the outskirts of Pennington, when he touched her hand, telling her they were almost home.

'You look very pale,' he said, frowning, as they drew up outside the house in Beaufort Crescent.

'I do feel a bit seedy,' she admitted. 'I shouldn't have let myself doze. I always feel worse afterwards.'

Rufus unlocked the front door, then picked her up. 'It's tradition to carry the bride over the threshold,' he said tersely as she stared at him in surprise. 'But in this case I think it's very necessary. You look ghastly, Jo.'

One look in her dressing-table mirror proved he was right when Rufus, panting slightly, set her on her feet in her new bedroom. 'If you don't mind I think I'll try out my beautiful new bed,' she said, and sat down abruptly on the edge of it.

Rufus looked down at her, frowning again, then slid off her shoes and unbuttoned the jacket of the new suit he'd bought for her only the day before. Dismayed to find she lacked the energy to help, Jo made no protest as he removed her silk shirt and the crimson wool skirt.

'Can you manage the rest yourself?' he asked, a pulse throbbing at the corner of his mouth.

Jo nodded dumbly.

Rufus strode to the door. 'I'll come back in a minute and see how you are. I'll make some tea.'

'Thank you,' she whispered, feeling worse by the minute.

Jo's fingers were like a set of ten thumbs as she took off her underwear, then slid naked under the brand-new lace-edged covers, desperate to lie down. If this was morning sickness, she thought irritably, its timing was a bit out. She looked up as Rufus came into the room with her suitcases.

'Could you fish out my dressing gown and a night-dress, please?' she asked him. 'They're in the smaller one.'

Rufus complied in silence. 'Can you manage?' he said shortly.

Jo shook her head unhappily. 'Sorry to be so feeble, but I don't think I can. I feel giddy—and I need to go to the bathroom.'

Rufus sat her upright, slid a nightgown over her head, then helped her out of the bed. Jo leaned against him for support, feeling sweat break out on her forehead. Without a word Rufus picked her up, carried her to the bathroom, waited outside for as long as necessary, then carried her back to the bed and laid her against the pillows.

'Sorry to be a nuisance,' she said, with an effort. 'I'll try not to make it a habit.'

He drew the covers over her, looking grim. 'Lie still. I'll bring you some tea.'

'Thank you.'

Jo lay very still indeed, so afraid to move that she breathed shallowly, dismayed to feel her whole body dewed with perspiration. Then pain struck, low in her stomach, and she groaned and sank her teeth into her bottom lip, panting.

'*Jo*—what is it?' said Rufus in consternation as he came into the room. He dumped the tray on the dressing table and crossed the room in a couple of strides.

'Pain,' gasped Jo, and waved a hand at her stomach. 'Feel sick. Help me—sit—up.'

When Rufus manoeuvred her gingerly to a sitting position, Jo promptly fainted dead away in his arms. She regained consciousness to the sound of his frantic voice calling her name, and tried to smile up into his haggard face.

'Pain in my stomach,' she got out with difficulty. 'I feel sick too.' Her eyes widened as pure agony clutched her like a vice.

Rufus laid her back with shaking hands and snatched at the telephone on the bedside table. 'I'll call the doctor!'

Dimly, through waves of sheer pain, she heard Rufus explaining that his wife was about six weeks pregnant and in great pain, then he rang off and dialled again, this time for an ambulance.

'Ambulance? Rufus, I don't need—' Then more
agony cut off her protests and Jo was engulfed in a
nightmare of pain which seemed to last for an un-
bearably long time until the doctor arrived, followed
a minute or two later by two paramedics in green uni-
forms. Rufus helped her answer several personal
questions while she was secured to a stretcher and
carried down to a waiting ambulance, where a drip
was attached to her arm with despatch.

'Am I losing the baby?' she gasped, and turned im-
ploring eyes on Rufus, who held her free hand tightly
and soothed her in a steady, reassuring voice which
belied the look in his eyes as the ambulance sped to
Pennington General with blue lights flashing. By the
time they arrived the pain was so intense that everything was a blur as Jo was delivered to a team ready
and alerted for her arrival, and the last thing she saw
was Rufus' haggard white face before the prick of a
needle sent her deep into blessed oblivion.

Jo opened her eyes to a small, pretty room, and wondered for a hazy moment if she was in a hotel again.
She tried to move a hand and found it was attached
to a tube which was dripping blood into her veins.
Not a hotel, then.

She closed her eyes again for a minute, then tried
to move her other hand with no success. With infinite
care she turned her head on the pillow and to her surprise found Rufus asleep in a chair beside the bed,
his hand grasping hers so tightly that not even sleep
had relaxed it.

Jo looked at him dispassionately. He looked terrible. The olive tint of his skin looked yellowish above
the white of his rather creased shirt, and he needed a

shave. And had his hair looked quite so silvery when she saw him last? Jo thought for a moment. When *had* she seen him last? She tried to move and winced.

The discomfort in her stomach brought recollection back in an unwelcome tidal wave, and she closed her eyes to hold back tears which leaked beneath her lashes and slid down her face. She'd lost the baby, obviously. Such a silly way to put it—as though she'd been careless.

'Jo?' said Rufus quietly, and she opened her eyes to the raw pain in his as he leaned forward to look down into her face. 'How do you feel?' He mopped gently at her tears with a tissue.

'Sore,' she croaked.

He nodded, his mouth twisting. 'As well you might.' He looked round as a nurse came into the room.

'Hello, Mrs Grierson,' she said briskly. 'Let me check up on you. Would you like some water?'

Jo nodded, and the nurse propped her up a little on her pillows and held a beaker with a straw to her mouth. Jo swallowed the cool liquid gratefully, and would have liked more, but the nurse shook her head, smiling.

'No more for a while. I'll come back shortly.'

'What time is it?' asked Jo hoarsely, when they were alone.

Rufus looked at his watch. 'Just after ten p.m.'

'When did I get in here?'

'About one. You were operated on immediately, then you were in a recovery room for a while, and this evening they moved you in here.' Rufus ran a hand over his chin. 'Sorry about the stubble. I haven't been home yet.'

Jo looked at him. 'No dinner?'

'No.' He smiled bleakly. 'I wasn't hungry.'

She tried to smile back, but tears welled in her eyes instead. Rufus wiped them away again, and she looked at him forlornly.

'I had a miscarriage?'

'No.' His hand tightened on hers. 'Yours was an ectopic pregnancy, Jo. The fertilised egg stuck in the Fallopian tube, which ruptured.'

Her pale face whitened alarmingly, and he grasped her hand in alarm. 'What did they do to me?' she said wildly.

'They saved your life,' said Rufus, breathing in unsteadily. 'I know the gynaecologist who performed the operation, as it happens. He told me we were very lucky the rupture waited until we arrived back from London.'

'Lucky!' she repeated bitterly. 'Unlucky for you, Rufus. I know how much you wanted the baby.'

'I wanted you alive a hell of a sight more,' he said harshly.

Jo's eyes widened. 'You mean I could have died?'

'You were bleeding profusely into your abdomen. If things hadn't moved so swiftly—' He thrust a hand through his hair, looking ill.

'Go home and get some sleep, Rufus,' she said, mustering as firm a voice as she could. 'I'm obviously fine now—isn't that right, Nurse?' she asked as the woman came back into the room. 'I've just been telling my husband to go home to bed.'

'Good idea. Don't worry, Mr Grierson, we'll look after your wife. I'll sit with her tonight, so you get off to bed and come back in the morning. She'll look like a different person by then, I promise.' The nurse smiled at Rufus, who got up reluctantly.

'I suppose you're right. But I'll stay if you want me to,' he said to Jo.

'No. Eat something and get some rest.' She tried to smile. 'Would you ring my mother?'

'I already have. She'll be here tomorrow.' Rufus hesitated, then bent and kissed Jo's dry lips. 'Goodnight. I'll see you in the morning.'

'Goodnight.' She looked up into his face. 'You're too tired to drive—take a taxi, Rufus.'

He smiled. 'I'll have to. I came by ambulance, remember?'

Jo smiled back valiantly, but the moment the door closed on him she turned her face into the pillow and wept as though her heart would break.

The nurse mopped her up, and scolded kindly, and after a while Jo stopped crying and asked for another drink, managing to smile when she was promised tea.

'Sorry to be such a misery,' said Jo thickly. 'It's just that...'

'I know. But don't worry. Nothing to stop you having another baby.'

Jo brightened. 'Are you sure?'

'Mr Conway will be in to see you in the morning. He'll tell you all you want to know.'

After a restless, uncomfortable night Jo was grateful when the consultant came to visit her quite early next morning. After asking a few questions James Conway examined her, then settled himself on the chair beside her and explained not only what had happened to her, but the exact operation he'd performed.

The sister standing in attendance behind the consultant nodded sagely. 'You were fortunate Mr Conway was on hand in the hospital. Your condition was life-threatening, Mrs Grierson.'

James Conway smiled reassuringly. 'I'm sorry about the vertical scar—I couldn't take time to do a cosmetic bikini job. But I put things right, removed the ruptured tube, and once you've had enough blood you'll be up and about and back to normal far sooner than you think.'

Jo licked her dry lips. 'Mr Conway,' she said, dreading his answer, 'please be frank with me. Does this mean I can't have another child?'

'Good heavens, no,' he said cheerfully. 'It might not be quite as easy with only one tube, but you'll manage. Lots of women do. In no time at all you'll be coming to one of my antenatal clinics.'

Jo doubted this. She looked away. 'Was there anything I could have done, or not done,' she said carefully, 'to avoid what happened?'

'Nothing at all, my dear. One of nature's cruel little tricks, I'm afraid. Don't worry, it's unlikely to happen a second time.' He patted her hand, then got up and strode off to begin on his operating list for the day, his entourage in close pursuit.

Because Jo was in a private room there was no limit put on the number of visitors allowed to see her—something she had cause to regret by the end of the first day. Rufus arrived as soon as the morning round was over, and brought her an exquisite arrangement of autumn flowers, plus a supply of fresh nightgowns, her toilet things, a couple of novels and some magazines.

'No chocolates,' he said, smiling as he bent to kiss her cheek. 'How do you feel, Jo?'

'Better than last night,' she assured him. 'And once they finish pumping blood into me I'll feel better still, I'm told.'

'I had a word with James Conway,' he said, sitting down. He took her hand in his and smoothed the back of it with a long finger. 'He put me in the picture. Said there's no reason why you can't have children in the normal way in future.' His eyes met hers. 'Though after what you went through I imagine the last thing you want is to make the attempt.'

They exchanged a long, unwavering look, then Jo turned her head away. 'The flowers are lovely. Thank you, Rufus.'

'Is there anything else you need?'

'No. You've thought of everything.'

Rufus stood up, looking pale and drawn above the dark, formal suit. 'I need to put in an hour or so in chambers, but I'll be back later.'

She nodded listlessly. 'Thank you.'

'You've nothing to thank me for, Jo.' His mouth twisted. 'Quite the contrary.'

At which point Rose Fielding arrived, and after a quick exchange of greetings Rufus excused himself and went off.

After embracing her daughter Rose Fielding sat down beside the bed, anxious to know every detail of what happened. 'I've told Thalia and Callie, of course, but staved off a visit from them until you feel better. They were all for coming with me this morning, but I vetoed that.' She took Jo's hand. 'Obviously I had to tell them about the baby, darling.'

'It's all right, Mother,' said Jo wearily. 'It's hardly a secret any more.' Tears slid down her cheeks again, and she mopped them up hurriedly. 'Funny, isn't it? At one time I could never cry. Now I can't stop.'

'I shouldn't try. Let it out, darling.' The hand tightened. 'You really wanted the baby, didn't you?'

Jo nodded miserably. 'And now Rufus is stuck with a wife he only married because he got her pregnant. What a mess.'

Mrs Fielding looked stunned. 'Is that how Rufus feels too?'

'How do I know, Mother?' said Jo irritably. 'It's impossible to know what Rufus feels, ever.'

'He was in a terrible state when he rang me last night. Totally distraught.'

Jo nodded morosely. 'Probably felt he'd murdered me.'

'*Murdered* you?'

'Apparently I could have died.'

'An ectopic pregnancy is nobody's fault, Jo.'

'I know. But he considers it his fault I was pregnant at all, ectopic or otherwise.'

'And was it?' said Mrs Fielding gently.

Jo turned heavy eyes on her mother. 'No. I'll spare you the intimate details, but it was my fault as much as his. I never imagined—' She broke off, biting her lip, and stared at the flowers Rufus had brought her.

Rose Fielding got up and began to unpack the bulging carrier bag she'd brought with her. 'Thalia sent you one of those sex-and-shopping novels and Callie's sending flowers. I've brought you a cookery book.'

Jo smiled reluctantly. 'A cookery book! In hospital?'

'I thought you could swot up some recipes to try out on Rufus when you get home.' Rose Fielding gave her daughter a wry smile. 'Or did you imagine that now there's no baby Rufus would send you post-haste back to your attic to resume a life of single blessedness?'

Since that, in essence, was exactly what Jo had pictured as her future she burst into tears again, and this time her mother took her in her arms and held her close until the storm was over.

The Griersons came to see Jo shortly afterwards, full of good wishes from Rory and Susannah, and both of them so concerned and sympathetic that Jo felt less embarrassed than expected over the pregnancy which had been kept secret from them. George Grierson stayed only a few minutes, but his wife settled down with Rose for a comfortable chat. Jo listened in amusement as between them the two women sorted her life out for her. By the time they left she'd been told that another baby was the best remedy possible to help her get over the first one, and Rufus would be ordered to see to it as soon as Jo recovered.

'I gather my mother's been trampling all over your sensibilities,' said Rufus when he visited her that evening. 'Sorry about that. She means well.'

'My mother was in complete agreement,' Jo assured him.

'You look better tonight,' he observed, relieved.

'Apparently I'll be almost as good as new in a day or two.'

'I doubt that,' he said crisply. 'When you come home I want you to take it easy for a while.'

'Mother brought me a cookery book,' said Jo evasively. 'Apparently I'm to swot up on it in here so I can delight you with all sorts of new dishes when I get home.'

Rufus gave her a smile of genuine amusement for the first time since their honeymoon. 'She's quite a lady, your mother. She wouldn't come and stay with me, you know, nor with my parents.'

'It's nothing personal. She's like me. Needs her space. She's got a list of old chums to visit, and she can invite them back if she's at my place.' Jo smiled at him. 'She works hard at being a trouble-free mother-in-law, Rufus. Hates to think she's being a nuisance.'

'She could never be that,' he said, and got up to look at her selection of literature. A bookmark protruded from one of the thrillers he'd brought her. 'Is it good?'

'Very. My concentration isn't what it might be, but I'm enjoying it.'

'Is there anything else you need?'

'No.' Jo braced herself. 'Would you sit down, Rufus? I'll be discharged in a couple of days. Before then we must talk.'

Rufus sat down, his eyes expressionless. 'What did you want to discuss, Jo?'

'Our future.'

'Go on.'

'Well—I know you married me because I was expecting your baby.' Jo cleared her throat. 'I'm not any more, so I'd quite understand if you felt you saw no reason to be married to me any more.'

He eyed her expressionlessly. 'Let me see if I've got this right. Now you're not pregnant any more you feel we should separate before we've even begun to be married?'

Jo's eyes fell. 'I thought,' she said rather desperately, 'that you might not want us to be tied together—now there's no need, I mean.'

'Did you really? Is that how *you* feel?' he added politely.

Since all she longed for was to be married to Rufus for the rest of her life Jo shook her head and looked away, afraid he would read her mind. 'No. It isn't.'

'Good,' said Rufus, leaning forward. He put a hand under her chin and turned her face to his. 'I object—violently—to the idea of a bride who leaves me flat before she's even had time to be my wife. Since we are married, Jocasta Grierson, I don't feel I'm being unreasonable in expecting you to return home with me once you're well enough, and proceed in exactly the same way we intended before events overtook us.'

Jo gazed at him in silence, her heart beating so loudly that she was surprised he couldn't hear it. 'Is that really what you want?'

'Yes, it is,' he said shortly, and got up. 'James Conway says I can take you home the day after tomorrow. In the interim I advise you to get used to the idea.' He stood looking down at her, his face stern beneath the silvered bronze hair. 'My one rash act caused you a great deal of suffering, Jo. But if it's any consolation I suffered too.'

'Did you?'

'Is that so surprising?' Rufus breathed in deeply, his eyes bitter. 'Put yourself in my place for a moment. In the beginning, that first night, I lost control and made you pregnant, then in London, though I gave you my word I would not, I made love to you again and *this* happened—'

'But not because we made love,' said Jo urgently. 'Nothing *made* it happen, nor could anything have prevented it. Mr Conway made that very clear.'

'He made it clear to me too,' said Rufus bleakly. 'Which doesn't alter the fact that you could have died as a result of my attentions, one way and another.'

'Rubbish,' said Jo scornfully. 'Is that why you want us to stay married? Because you feel guilty?'

'No, it's not.' He looked at her very steadily. 'I went to great lengths beforehand, Jo, to give the impression that we got married purely because we wanted to spend our lives together. I'm human enough to want to preserve the fiction.' His eyes glittered suddenly. 'And this is where I use emotional blackmail. Fate cut short my first marriage, Jo. When you were rushed into hospital I thought it was going to happen again. But it didn't. So I assume *our* marriage is meant to last a while.'

CHAPTER NINE

BECAUSE Jo had rarely been ill in her life once the usual childish ailments were over, her slow return to normal annoyed her intensely. The scar healed well, the soreness subsided gradually and her blood count was pronounced satisfactory, but she felt tired and listless, and, worst of all to Jo, was plagued by a tendency to tears. Hormones, she told herself, and took enormous care to prevent the tears getting the better of her in company with Rufus, who was adamant she needed rest.

'Try not to overdo things,' he ordered her.

'I'm strong as a horse normally.'

'This isn't normally. My mother keeps telling me you need cosseting.'

'What a lovely word!'

'You'd be cosseted to death if my mother had her way,' he warned, grinning. 'Now Rose has gone back, Mother would be here all day long, given half the chance, force-feeding you egg-nog and beef tea.'

'How sweet of her,' said Jo, touched. 'But if that's why you're dashing home at regular intervals all the time you needn't. I'm fine on my own.'

'You want me out of the way so you can get back to your computer,' he said accusingly.

'No.' Jo looked away. 'I don't want you out of the way.'

'Good.' He paused as though waiting for her to say more, then went to the door. 'I'll see to dinner.'

'I can do that—'

'No, you can't. Not yet.' Rufus gave her his mad-deningly superior smile. 'Besides, I didn't say I was *cooking* it; I'm having it sent over from that new Italian restaurant.'

Sharing a house—and her life—with Rufus proved far less stressful than Jo expected. Little by little she discovered she had more in common with him in many ways than she'd had with Claire, which made her feel guilty. Though less guilty now there was no baby. Nor was there likely to be. The second Mrs Grierson slept alone in her handsome bed.

In spite of Rufus' deep disapproval Jo began working on the draft of her novel as soon as she felt well enough, helped enormously by the fact that Rufus asked his mother's cleaner to lend a hand at Beaufort Crescent two mornings a week.

'If you must get back to your computer at least let me smooth your path a little,' said Rufus. 'Now Rory's left home Mother doesn't need Dolly every day.'

Help in the house was a new departure for Jo. Such a luxury had never featured in her mother's household, though both Thalia and Callie had a 'little woman'. Dolly, as Mrs Beryl Dalton was known to the Griersons, was anything but little. She was a tall, heavily built woman with boundless energy and good humour, and got through the housework at such speed that she had time over to do the ironing or peel veg-etables, or whatever else she found to occupy her before she went home, including making soup for Jo's lunch.

Life assumed a pleasant, livable routine, and two months into her semi-detached but surprisingly amicable marriage Jo professed herself as satisfied with her novel as she was ever going to be.

'Polishing it up has taken so much longer than I expected,' she told Rufus over dinner that night.

He looked up. 'Hardly surprising in the circumstances.'

'Actually,' said Jo with care, 'having the novel to work on was a big help. With my convalescence, I mean.'

'Once I laid down the law!'

'You were a pig,' she said, eyes kindling. 'Just because I was still at my computer when you came home a couple of evenings—'

'Only because you looked hellishly tired!' Rufus eyed her dispassionately. 'You still do sometimes. Take a break once you've sent your manuscript off.'

'I probably will, for a bit,' she assured him, swallowing resentment at his tone. 'Though the next story's already mulling round in my mind. Don't worry,' she added hastily at the look he gave her. 'I've got lots of research to do before I actually start writing again.'

'I'm pleased to hear it,' he said drily. 'When do you go back to James Conway?'

'Tomorrow.' Jo looked down at her plate. 'Hardly necessary, really; I feel perfectly well.'

He stretched out a hand and caught her wrist. 'But you'll go,' he stated.

Jo nodded, resigned. 'Yes, I'll go.'

Jo parcelled up her novel and sent it off to Diadem with something of a wrench, as though part of herself had been posted with it. Afterwards she drove off to keep her appointment with James Conway. The gynaecologist gave her a thorough examination, pronounced himself satisfied with her recovery and told her to carry on with her life normally, both in the bedroom and out of it. Jo thanked him and hurried home, glad that the consultant had no idea that life in her particular bedroom was a very solitary one. Rufus had rarely crossed the threshold since the day of her mad rush to the hospital.

Without the routine at her computer to shape her days, Jo felt at a loose end for a while. But gradually she evolved a new daily programme. Afternoons were kept for research, but in the mornings she walked round to Elizabeth Grierson's for coffee or went Christmas shopping with her. Some days she met Susannah for lunch during her sister-in-law's break from her job as fashion buyer at one of the town's large department stores, and Jo also paid regular visits to the flat in Bruton Road to make sure all was well. But she had no inclination to return there to work. It seemed sensible to stop paying the rent, but Jo couldn't quite bring herself to burn her boats entirely.

'I had a letter from Diadem today,' she told Rufus one night.

'Already? What did they say?'

'It was just a receipt for the manuscript.' She smiled wryly. 'My heart did a somersault when I saw the Diadem logo—it was a horrible let-down.'

He smiled. 'You probably won't hear for a while yet.'

'It's bound to be rejected,' she said, sighing, then grinned philosophically. 'Not that I'll let that put me off. I'll keep trying until I get lucky.'

Eventually Jo stopped lying in wait for the postman and turned her attention to Christmas arrangements.

The previous Christmas the entire Fielding family, including Jo's father, had celebrated Christmas with Thalia and Charlie in their elegant apartment. This year both Thalia and Callie were committed to Christmas with their respective in-laws, and were making their mother's life a misery with their worry over her yule arrangements. Jo shut them up by telling them she'd taken it for granted their mother would come to Beaufort Crescent for the festive season, and was invited to accompany Rufus and herself to the Griersons' for Christmas dinner.

Rose Fielding thanked her youngest daughter with rapture. 'Now perhaps the girls will get off my back,' she said in relief.

'Apparently Christmas is a big thing in the Grierson household,' Jo told her mother. 'It should be fun.'

'How very kind of Elizabeth. I'll write a little note. And I'd love to come to you, Jo,' said Rose, 'but on one condition. I sleep in your flat.'

'Oh, *Mother*,' said Jo, exasperated. 'There's plenty of space here—the guest room's never been used.'

'It's nice to be invited, but you know what I'm like. Humour me. Now then, how are you—really?'

'I'm fine. Mr Conway discharged me last time as perfectly fit.'

'Good. Do you agree with his verdict?'

'Oh, yes—except for deep depression when the postman doesn't deliver a letter from Diadem.'

But there was no news from Diadem before Christmas, which was a feast celebrated with much enthusiasm in the senior Grierson household. Rufus collected Rose Fielding mid-morning from Jo's flat so that the three of them could open their presents together over a light early lunch before joining the

Griersons for Christmas dinner. While he was gone Jo stoked up the fire Rufus had lit first thing in the sitting room, savouring the short interval to herself before the day began in earnest.

She stared into the flickering flames, looking back over the first weeks of the marriage which, against all odds, was proving remarkably successful. Jo's face shadowed as she mourned for the baby who had never arrived, but after a few moments of reverie she counted her blessings, and went to make coffee, ready for her mother's arrival.

Later the three of them set off together for the party, Rufus in all the glory of Jo's gift of a Chinese silk waistcoat and Rose Fielding draped with a vast silk scarf of the same provenance.

'How did you know I yearned for gold hoops, Rufus?' said Jo, admiring her reflection in the hall mirror before they went out to the car.

'I can read your mind,' he whispered in her ear, looking a lot different from the haggard, distraught man who'd rushed her to hospital only a few weeks before.

'I must remember to think pure thoughts,' she said, laughing.

'Spoilsport.'

Elizabeth Grierson gathered not only her immediate family to her bosom on Christmas Day, but several elderly relatives who had nowhere else to go for the festivities, plus Susannah's parents and young sister, and the young man from next door, who was home alone for Christmas because his parents were visiting his sister in Australia.

It was an odd mix but a successful one, with a lavish, traditional meal followed by an evening devoted to uproarious games. Jo joined in with enthusiasm, utterly fascinated to discover a new, roistering side to her husband when it was his turn to act out one of the titles his mother had thought up earlier.

Rufus studied the folded slip he'd taken from the basket presided over by his great-aunt, then took centre stage and indicated in dumb show that his was a song title. Rufus took off his jacket and tie, lowered his eyelids, cast a sultry look round the room, strummed on an imaginary guitar and revolved his pelvis in a way which brought roars of laughter and catcalls from his audience, including Jo, who was entranced by the sight of her husband playing the fool. Then he held up three fingers to signal three words and started on the first one by kneeling in front of Jo, hands clasped over his heart.

'Love!' called Susannah promptly, and Rufus nodded, grinning, then pointed to himself for the second word.

'Me,' said everyone in unison, then Rufus slid his arms round his startled wife, smoothing the shining dark head cradled against his shoulder, and immediately the older element in the room bawled, '"Love Me Tender"'!'

Rufus bowed theatrically but stayed where he was, keeping his arm round Jo, where it was to remain for the rest of the evening. 'Did you like my Elvis impersonation?' he asked as Susannah took centre stage for the next title.

'Masterly,' she said, giggling. 'I'd no idea you were such a ham!'

'Hidden talents,' he whispered, his smile touching off a small, hopeful flame which burned steadily inside her for the rest of the night.

It was one in the morning before they arrived home.

'What's the matter?' Rufus asked as he took Jo's coat.

Cursing her husband's skill in reading her mind, she assured him that she was fine and would be even better after a cup of tea.

Rufus followed her into the kitchen, leaning against a counter while Jo busied herself with kettle and tea things. 'You were in tearing spirits right up until we left, but now you're not. What was your mother talking about in the back of the car? I didn't ask in case it was something private. Was it bad news of some kind?'

Jo poured boiling water into the teapot, put the lid on and stood staring at it, willing unwanted tears to stay put. 'No,' she said gruffly. 'Quite the opposite, really. Callie's expecting a baby.'

'And you mind.' Rufus turned her to face him and drew her close, smoothing a hand over her hair as she buried her face against him.

Jo made a heroic attempt to control her tears, and at last drew away with a damp, shaky smile. 'That waistcoat was expensive. I don't want to ruin it.'

Rufus promptly stripped off both jacket and waistcoat and returned her to her former place. 'You need more cosseting.'

She gave a chuckle too much like a sob for her own liking at the memory of another night when she'd cried into his shirt-front. 'Such a lovely word! Sorry to spoil your evening, Rufus.'

'You haven't.' He put her away from him slightly. 'You're tired. Go up and get into bed. I'll bring your tea.'

'Thank you,' she said hoarsely, and tore a sheet of kitchen paper from its roll. She mopped her face vigorously and gave him a smile. 'To think that once upon a time I never cried over anything!'

Jo went upstairs to undress, and wrapped herself afterwards in the flagrantly luxurious dressing gown Rufus had given her that morning, enjoying the feel of the scarlet cashmere. She creamed her face and brushed her hair, then sat on her elegant bed, propped up against the pillows.

Rufus paused on the threshold, arrested, then brought the mug to the table beside her, his face rigidly blank. 'You look very—festive. I thought it would suit you.'

'I wasn't sure whether it made me look like Father Christmas or a scarlet woman,' she said, flippant to disguise her nerves.

'Definitely not the former,' he assured her, then stood very still as she held her arms up to him.

'Rufus,' she said breathlessly, 'could you possibly cosset me a tiny bit more before you go to bed? It *is* Christmas.'

For a split second Jo thought he would refuse her, then with an odd, choked sound Rufus pulled her off the bed and into his arms, crushing his mouth down on hers like a man starved for the touch and taste of her. She locked her hands behind his neck, and gave him back kiss for kiss until they were breathing in ragged, painful gasps, both of them furiously impatient with shirt buttons and the satin girdle that knotted in Rufus' frantic hands before he managed to undo it and thrust the gown from her shoulders. He breathed in sharply when he found her naked beneath it and bent his head, his mouth hot in the hollow between her breasts as his hands caressed her. She gasped and clenched her chattering teeth, and he sank to his knees, his mouth like a brand against the satiny skin of her waist as he thrust the gown aside and let it fall to the floor.

Suddenly Rufus was still, and she opened her eyes to find him staring at the scar. He leapt to his feet and backed away, and Jo snatched up her dressing gown and wrapped herself in it with trembling fingers, feeling as though he'd punched her in the stomach.

'Oh, God—I'm sorry,' he said harshly. 'I'd forgotten. Jo, I can't—'

'No. Of course. I quite understand.' Jo turned her back and leaned both hands on the dressing table. 'Please go.'

'Jo, listen,' he urged hoarsely, but she shook her head.

'Get *out*, Rufus!' she said with violence, suddenly at the end of her tether.

In the mirror she saw his hands reach for her, then fall, and Rufus turned on his heel and went out, closing the door behind him with enormous care.

Fortunately Rose Fielding was leaving next day to spend Boxing Day with an old friend before returning to Willowdene Lodge. It would have been more than Jo could bear to keep up a whole day of pretence in front of her mother. For the half-hour the three of them spent together over coffee, discussing the riotous day before, Jo kept up appearances with remarkable

ease, including Rufus in the conversation so naturally
that all could have been normal.

They saw Rose off together, arm in arm, told her
to drive with care and waved her out of sight, then
Jo wrenched her hand away and went back in the
house, deliberately ignoring Rufus. Without a word
she went straight upstairs to shut herself in her room.
Once inside she leaned against the door for a moment
or two, eyes closed, then squared her shoulders and
sat down at her desk. Summoning concentration by
force of will, Jo read through the notes she'd made,
then switched on her computer, blanked Rufus from
her mind, and began to type the opening paragraph
of her new novel.

At midday Rufus knocked and came into the room
with a tray containing a pot of tea and some sandwiches from the ham Jo had roasted on Christmas
Eve. She badly wanted to snarl at him, tell him she
wasn't hungry and didn't want his rotten sandwiches.
But the combination of stress and hard work had
made her ravenous, so she thanked Rufus with deep-
frozen courtesy, waited in pointed silence until he left
the room, then fell on the food while she read through
her morning's work. Rufus brought her tea at one
stage in the afternoon, reminded her that they were
due to dine with Rory and Susannah that evening, but
otherwise made no attempt to make her talk to him.
Jo assured herself she was glad. And although it was
Boxing Day, and not New Year's Eve, she made a
resolution never, ever to cry again. Tears turned her
into a crazy, pathetic creature who craved comfort.
Even so, it had taken enormous effort to reach out
to Rufus the night before. And for a few, electrifying

minutes his response had been gloriously, passionately gratifying.

Jo shuddered, willing her mind to concentrate on the fictional character she was creating, blocking out thoughts of the look in his eyes as he'd stared at her scar. Any other husband would have seen it long since, of course, and grown used to it gradually as it healed. But one look had repelled *her* husband so much that he couldn't bear to touch her. Rufus Grierson, she thought bitterly, required perfection. He liked his women flawless in every way. Like Claire.

CHAPTER TEN

IT WAS February before Jo heard anything more from Diadem. The wait made life even more trying from her own point of view. Of Rufus' viewpoint she knew nothing, since she pointedly didn't ask for it, and after one or two abortive attempts to bridge the sudden gulf between them neither did he.

After the humiliation of his rejection Jo gave up sharing any meal with Rufus other than the nightly trial of dinner. She took to keeping a tea-tray in her bedroom so she could breakfast on biscuits and tea in solitude, unable to cope early in the day with the armed truce their marriage had become. When her husband knocked on her bedroom door early one morning, therefore, Jo was surprised. Rufus usually departed for his chambers without communication.

'Come in,' said Jo, eyeing her husband questioningly as he came in dressed ready for the day, his pinstriped suit a dark grey which matched the marks under his eyes. Rufus, it seemed, slept no better than she did these days. He came over to the bed, holding out a letter.

'It's from Diadem. I thought you'd like it straight away.' He raised an eyebrow, smiling. 'And I want to know what they say.'

'Thank you,' said Jo, accepting it gingerly as though it might bite her.

'It's an envelope,' he pointed out, 'not a returned manuscript.'

'True.' Jo managed a smile. 'But I'm still afraid to open it.'

'Perhaps you'd rather do it in private,' he said instantly, and turned to go.

'No!' she said urgently. 'No, of course not, Rufus. I'm being silly.' She slid a fingernail under the flap and took out a letter. She read it through in silence, then read it through again, just in case she'd made a mistake.

'Well?' demanded Rufus impatiently. 'The suspense is killing me. What does it say?'

Jo handed him the letter, looking dazed. 'They like it—or at least they will do after it's been revised a bit.'

Rufus read it through, then gave her the first real smile she'd seen on his face since Christmas. 'This is wonderful news, Jo. Congratulations.'

He moved towards her involuntarily, but checked himself, and instead of kissing her as she'd hoped he handed Jo her letter.

'They want me to go down to London to lunch next week,' she said quickly, to hide her disappointment.

'You'll enjoy that.' He glanced at his watch, and sighed. 'I must go. I'm late.' He looked down at her. 'Jo—let's go out for a celebration dinner tonight. We can't let the occasion go unmarked.'

Jo looked at him for a moment, then nodded. 'Thank you. I'd like that.'

'I'll arrange it. Anywhere in particular?'

She smiled a little. 'Yes. The Mitre. I haven't been back there since—since we got married. I can tell them the glad news.'

'Right.' He went to the door, then turned. 'Jo, once you've spoken to your mother, ring mine with your news. She'd like to know.'

'I was going to anyway, Rufus.'

'Yes, of course.' He paused, as though taking pleasure in the sight of her as she sat propped up against pillows, her hair hanging dark and tousled on her shoulders. 'You look better, Jo.'

Better than what? she thought, and smiled politely. 'Thank you.'

'I'll see you tonight,' he said, and closed the door behind him.

Jo stared at it disconsolately for a moment or two, wishing she could call him back, ask him to stay, share her triumph a little longer. Then she looked at the letter from Diadem again and gave a delighted little wriggle of elation as she picked up the telephone beside her bed.

'Mother? Guess what!'

Jo spent a disgracefully long time on the phone. She basked in the congratulations and praise heaped on her by her mother, promised to take Rufus down to lunch the following Sunday, then rang her mother-in-law, who was equally euphoric, and begged to pass the glad news on to Susannah. If only, thought Jo wistfully, she could have told Claire.

When she was dressed she braced herself to ring Gloria Beaumont, thinking it would be unkind to let Claire's mother find out from someone else. It was not a task she relished. Claire's mother had never quite been able to come to terms with the fact that Rufus had married again at all, let alone chosen Jo Fielding to succeed her adored, matchless Claire.

Mrs Beaumont congratulated Jo perfunctorily, plainly not very interested in news of the novel. Almost immediately she began to talk of Claire and how much she still missed her beloved child. 'Rufus does too,' she added. 'He told me so only the other day. He loved her so very desperately, you know.'

'Yes, I do know,' said Jo quietly. 'I miss her too.'

'Of course you do. I must be grateful poor dear Rufus has you to turn to for comfort.'

When Jo finally managed to put an end to the conversation she slumped on the side of her bed, all her pleasure in the day spoiled. Then the phone rang and she brightened when she heard Susannah's jubilant voice demanding Jo meet her in town for lunch to celebrate.

Jo had taken to Susannah from the moment they'd first met. Rory's wife was an outgoing creature who loved her husband, and her job, and got on well with most people. And she had never met Claire. In this instance, at least, there were no comparisons for Jo to live up to, and she'd quickly grown very fond of Susannah.

'Jo!' Susannah came hurrying out from the perfumed interior of the store and gave Jo a hug. 'Who's a clever girl, then? Let's go and eat something sinful and fattening to celebrate.'

After Mrs Beaumont's reaction Susannah's jubilation was balm to Jo, and she said so quite frankly. 'I need to let off steam with someone.'

'You look better for it too,' said Susannah, and bit her lip. 'I've been a bit worried, Jo. Rory, too.'

Jo met the anxious brown eyes squarely. 'Because you think things are strained between Rufus and me?'

Susannah let out a sigh of relief. 'Well, yes. But I'm glad you said it, not me.'

'It's been hard to adjust,' said Jo with difficulty.

'Since losing the baby?'

'Yes. And I'm Rufus' second wife, remember.' Jo smiled brightly. 'It's not the same kind of thing as you and Rory.'

'It looked like it at Christmas!' The other girl heaved a sigh. 'But since then it's obvious neither of you is very happy these days. We—we worry.'

Jo smiled ruefully. 'And I thought we were putting on such a brave face to the world.'

'You are. It's what goes on behind the masks that worries us!' Susannah put out a hand, and Jo clasped it. 'Rory's taking me to the theatre tonight, otherwise I'd suggest we went out to dinner to celebrate.'

'Rufus is taking me to the Mitre, so I can boast to all my old pals.'

'Oh, brilliant. Have a really lovely time.' Susannah smiled cajolingly. 'And please make it up with Rufus, Jo.'

Easier said than done, thought Jo later, as she got ready for the evening. By the time Rufus came home she was ready in the black cashmere dress her sisters had clubbed together to give her for Christmas. Thalia and Callie never stopped trying to improve her appearance, thought Jo affectionately as she viewed the finished result in the hall mirror, but their taste, as always, was impeccable. The dress clung flatteringly in all the right places. She fastened the gold hoops in her ears, and surveyed the result critically just as Rufus came through the front door carrying an enormous bunch of tawny roses.

They both spoke at once, then stopped, smiling at each other.

'I'll go first because I must tell you at once how beautiful you look,' said Rufus, and handed her the roses. 'For my talented wife.'

'Why, thank you, Rufus,' she said, touched.

'I brought them home at lunchtime,' he said, surprising her. 'When I found you were out I took them back again.'

'You could have left them with a note.'

'I preferred to present them in person.'

Having started on such a harmonious note, the evening was more of a success than Jo had expected, after the weeks of frosted, barely civil coexistence. Her choice of the Mitre for dinner was inspired. Because Rufus had told Phil Dexter the good news Jo was given red-carpet treatment from the moment she arrived. She was hugged, kissed and bombarded with congratulations, then served with champagne before and during dinner, which was excellent, as always at the Mitre.

'Perhaps I can get a toast in now,' said Rufus drily, when they were left to eat their main course in relative peace. He raised his glass, his eyes warm as they smiled into hers. 'To Jocasta Fielding, and the success she richly deserves.'

Jo acknowledged the toast with gratitude. 'Thank you, Rufus.' Her eyes danced suddenly. 'If I sell well enough, and Diadem want a follow-up, things could change a lot in the future.'

His face drained of animation. 'In what way?'

'I might make so much money, you could retire and be a kept man!' She eyed him searchingly. 'Why the poker-face, Rufus?'

'I thought you meant something quite different.'

'What, exactly?'

He abandoned his meal and leaned back in his chair, his eyes hard to read in the discreet lighting of the Mitre's dining room. 'That you might want to leave Pennington. And me,' he added without emotion.

Jo laid down her knife and fork, aligning them on her half-full plate with finicking precision, keeping her eyes on the task. 'Is that what *you* want?' she asked very quietly, her words almost drowned by the buzz of general conviviality in the restaurant.

'No, I do not!' He leaned forward. 'Look at me, Jo. Let's bring this out into the open. The last few weeks have been hellish. For me, at least.'

Her eyes flashed. 'I haven't enjoyed them much either.'

'I know that.' He held out his hand, and after a moment she put hers into it. 'Jo, I know you would never have married me if I hadn't forced your hand. But until Christmas we were getting along reasonably well together.' Rufus smiled a little. 'You're very easy to live with.'

'So are you,' she admitted, and gave him a sudden, mischievous grin. 'Much to my astonishment.'

He sobered, his fingers tightening on hers. 'You haven't shown much pleasure in the arrangement lately.'

'Can you blame me?' she asked quietly.

'If you're referring to the episode at Christmas—'

'Of course I am, but I'd rather not again. Tonight or ever,' she said flatly. She lifted her chin. 'If you want to revert to our pre-Christmas relationship, Rufus, I'm in full agreement. But you're a man, and a very attractive one, and I quite understand how difficult it is for you—'

'I doubt it,' he broke in sardonically, and raised an eyebrow, keeping tight hold of the hand she tried to pull away. 'But I'm not perfectly clear as to your drift. Are you saying you'll turn a blind eye if I satisfy my male urges elsewhere occasionally?'

Jo's eyes gleamed dangerously. 'No way. I'm saying I'll be perfectly happy to divorce you if you do.'

'Will you really? And does this code of behaviour work both ways?' he enquired silkily. 'How about your libidinous urges?'

'In my life they happen once in a blue moon,' she said tartly, and tugged her hand free. 'They're unlikely to pose a problem.'

'So if I agree to quell mine you're willing to stay married to me?'

It wasn't what she wanted at all, but it was a start. Perhaps in time... Jo nodded. 'Yes, I suppose so.'

'Any more enthusiasm like that and I'll get above myself!'

She smiled. 'But seriously, Rufus, I meant what I said. If you do want out I wouldn't be difficult about it.'

He looked at her narrowly. 'And if you want the same I assume I'm not required to be "difficult" either.'

'Exactly.' Jo spotted a waitress bearing down on them. 'I don't want anything else, Rufus. Can we go home now?'

From the night of the celebration dinner life reverted to the friendly companionship Jo and Rufus had shared before Christmas, so that Jo was in a far better frame of mind for several reasons when they went down to Willowdene Lodge the following Sunday for lunch with Rose Fielding. Thalia and Charlie were there to share in the celebrations, but Callie had rung Jo previously, warm with praise, excusing herself from the family lunch due to her temporary problem with the smell and taste of any food other than breakfast cereal.

Jo and Rufus drove home in the evening afterwards, discussing Jo's visit to Diadem.

'I'll buy you a train ticket tomorrow,' said Rufus as they drank coffee later at the kitchen table.

'I still can't believe it,' said Jo dreamily. 'It's an extraordinary feeling, to know someone might actually read—and enjoy—what I've written.'

'When do *I* get to read it?' he asked, smiling at her.

'When I get the first hardback copies. I want you to believe you're reading a proper book, not just your wife's outpourings.'

'You think of yourself as my wife, then?'

Jo flushed a little and drank down the rest of her coffee. 'Well, yes, I do.' She looked up to meet his eyes. 'You find that odd?'

Rufus shook his head. 'No. I'm—gratified.'

'You always choose your words so carefully, Rufus Grierson. Don't you ever say something spontaneous off the top of your head?'

'Never,' he said promptly, and raised an eyebrow. 'By the way, what do you intend to wear on Tuesday?'

'I'd like to be all nonchalant and say I haven't thought about it, but I have,' she said sheepishly. 'Any suggestions?'

'Yes. Buy yourself a new winter coat tomorrow— and wear it over that dress.' He wagged a long finger at her. 'So far you haven't used the credit card I sorted out for you.'

Which was deliberate on Jo's part. She'd felt so hostile towards Rufus since Christmas that she'd made sure she spent no money of his at all other than to buy food and pay Dolly.

'Right. I'll do that. Thank you,' she said, smiling at him. 'Fine feathers might boost my confidence.'

'Yours needs boosting?'

'About my looks, yes.' Jo pulled a face. 'I've always yearned to be tall and fair like—'

'Claire?' said Rufus quickly. 'It's time you put comparisons behind you.'

She looked at him levelly. 'Actually, I meant my sisters. Dad used to call me his little monkey-face and tease my mother about the milkman.' She yawned, and stood up. 'I'm for bed.'

'I am too,' said Rufus, and followed her out of the kitchen, turning off the lights behind them. 'So you'll go shopping for a coat tomorrow?' he said as they reached the door of her room.

Jo nodded. 'Not that I expect success. Coats tend to be cut with taller women in mind.'

Rufus chuckled. 'I'll take an hour off and come with you, if you like.'

'Goodness, no,' said Jo immediately. 'You'd be bored to tears. I'll enlist Susannah. She's the expert.'

'Yes, of course,' said Rufus without expression, and bent to kiss Jo's cheek, as he'd done every night since the cessation of hostilities between them. 'Goodnight.'

Jo had been in bed for some time before she hit upon something indefinable in Rufus' reaction to her refusal of his company on the shopping expedition.

He'd felt rebuffed, she thought, biting her lip. Had he *wanted* to come?

'Rufus,' she said without preamble, when he came in to say goodbye the following morning—another habit which marked the new phase in their relationship. 'I honestly thought you'd be bored by shopping for a coat. I didn't mean to offend you.'

'No, I know you didn't.' He stood looking down at her in amusement. 'Part of my reason for offering myself so nobly was as a curb on your well-known leaning towards economy.'

'What was the other part?' she asked curiously.

'I'll leave you to work that out for yourself,' he said, with his faint, maddening smile. He touched a long finger to her cheek. 'Now it's time I got to grips with Monday. See you tonight.'

Jo travelled down to London in confident mood, buoyed up by the knowledge that she looked her best in the black wool dress, worn under a thigh-length jacket in a wonderfully impractical shade of apricot which flattered her skin and looked warm in the cold light of a February day.

Susannah had been a great help, not only in suggesting clothes suited to Jo's colouring and lack of inches, but in following Rufus' instruction to see that his wife didn't economise on her choice. Fat chance, thought Jo with amusement. Susannah had steered her straight to the department which specialised in top designer labels, then bullied her into going the whole hog on new shoes and a bag for encore.

Jo took a taxi to the publishers, and met with a slight set-back to her newly boosted confidence. Miles Hay had gone down with flu, she was told, but one

of the other editors would take care of Mrs Grierson
if she wouldn't mind waiting a moment or two. Jo
was taken up in a lift and shown into an office with
a view over London rooftops, and after a short interval the door opened and a man strode into the
room, hand outstretched.

'Sorry to keep you waiting, Mrs Grierson...' He
stopped short as Jo got to her feet, his eyebrows
shooting up in astonishment. '*Jo?* I can't believe it!
Are *you* Jocasta Grierson?'

'Good heavens—Linus Cole!' Jo held out her hand,
but Linus swept her into his arms and kissed her
soundly on both cheeks.

'I never knew your name was Jocasta,' he declared,
smiling all over his clever, confident face.

'It's my dark secret,' she said, beaming. 'Gosh,
Linus, so you're with Diadem! I was supposed to see
a man called Miles Hay.'

'My boss. Miles is on his bed of pain as we speak—
though with the gorgeous Mrs Hay to comfort him
flu could have its compensations.' Linus looked sleek,
well dressed and very well fed, in vivid contrast to the
lean, hungry student she'd known in the past. He in-
stalled her in the comfortable chair in front of his
desk, then seated himself behind it, exuding pleasure
in the encounter. 'Well, well. So little Jo's our budding
author—and a married lady, to boot.' He eyed her
appreciatively. 'You look *wonderful*.'

Thanks to Rufus and Susannah, thought Jo in secret
amusement. 'So do you, Linus.'

From then on it was easy, as though the twelve-year
gap in their friendship had never existed, though Jo
laughed Linus to scorn when he swore he'd never forgotten her.

'Pull the other one! I've grown up a bit from the naïve little maiden you knew,' she said, smiling. 'I actually believed you'd sweep me off to Cambridge with you and live happily ever after.'

'Is that what you expected?' he said in astonishment. 'It never occurred to me.'

'No, I know very well it didn't, you rotter.' She smiled at him, pulling a face. 'But I'd better watch my Ps and Qs or you'll refuse to publish my novel.'

'No chance of that,' he assured her. 'Miles has already accepted it. My job is merely to help you cut and polish it. Don't worry—I'm good,' he assured her.

Jo had no doubt of it. Linus had been intellectually the most impressive man she'd ever met. Until Rufus Grierson.

It was a busy, productive day, with a delicious lunch at a fashionable restaurant, where the chef was a well-known television personality and came out of the kitchen to chat with Linus and his guest. Jo returned to Pennington that evening in a euphoric daze, clutching a manuscript annotated with suggestions on how to upgrade her original novel into the best-seller Miles Hay—and Linus—thought it was certain to be once she'd worked a little on it.

'How did it go?' said Rufus, when he met her at the station.

Jo grinned at him, eyes sparkling. 'I don't know whether I'm standing on my head or my heels. I've got a fair bit of revision to do on the manuscript, but nothing really fundamental. I'll give you all the details over dinner—not that I'm very hungry. I had rather a sumptuous lunch.'

Rufus bent to kiss her cheek. 'Let me order something in.'

'No need. I made a casserole yesterday. It just needs heating up. I promise I'll give you a blow-by-blow description of my day as we eat it, but at the moment all I can think of is a hot bath!'

They were sitting at the table in the kitchen Jo loved so much before she told Rufus the most amazing part of the day. While she'd enjoyed her bath Rufus had showered and changed into well-worn cords and a heavy sweater, and minus the dark circles under his eyes, with hair gleaming like newly polished silver under the central kitchen light, he looked formidably attractive.

Jo, her designer finery exchanged for a scarlet sweater and black jeans, stole a look at her husband as she served him with a generous portion of beef casseroled in a spiced wine sauce. How had she ever thought Linus Cole so irresistible? she thought in wonder. Linus' fair good looks were rather florid these days, and suffered badly in comparison with the lean planes of Rufus' face and the flat, skier's muscles of his tall body.

'I'm waiting,' said Rufus impatiently. 'Come out of your daydream and tell me what happened.'

Jo pulled herself together and launched into an account of her day, rueful about the amount of revision needed on the novel, but excited over the compliments about her writing. She gave Rufus a blow-by-blow description, but kept the pièce de résistance to the last.

'Miles Hay was ill with flu,' she said in conclusion, and grinned at him, her eyes sparkling. 'I was handed over to one of the other editors, and to my amazement it was Linus Cole—a man I used to know in college!'

Rufus' face took on the deadpan expression that Jo had learned to dread. 'Linus Cole,' he said slowly, eyes narrowed. 'The name rings a bell. If my memory serves me correctly you knew him *very* well. Wasn't he the object of your teenage passion?'

CHAPTER ELEVEN

Jo STARED at him in astonishment. 'Good heavens, Rufus, how on earth did you remember that?'

He shrugged, his eyes inscrutable. 'Claire was voluble on the subject.'

'How very boring for you,' said Jo, and jumped up. 'Would you like some cheese?'

'No, it wasn't boring, and no, I don't want any cheese.' Rufus caught her wrist, forcing her to look at him. 'Just for the record, Claire never bored me when she talked about you. She told me you were crazy about this Linus Cole of yours—'

'He's not mine,' she retorted, trying to pull away, but Rufus held her fast.

'But you wanted him to be!'

Jo looked down at his fingers on her wrist, and he released it, but kept hold of her hand, smoothing his thumb over the red marks he'd left on her skin. 'I was only eighteen, Rufus,' she said quietly. 'He was a postgraduate and a fair bit older than me. The males in my life up to that point had been my father and the boys at his school. Where men were concerned I was straight out of the egg. I was flattered when he fancied me. I was the envy of all my friends. Of course I was crazy about him.'

'Is he the reason why you sent the book to Diadem?' he demanded, deadpan no longer.

'No, he's not!' Jo wrenched her hand away and picked up their dinner plates. 'I merely did my homework. I sent my book to the publisher most likely to accept the kind of story I've written. I had no idea Linus worked for Diadem until today.'

Rufus eyed her in such blatant disbelief that Jo cleared away at top speed, deflated like a pricked balloon. When Rufus took the coffee-tray into the sitting room afterwards Jo was tempted to leave him alone with it. But the thought of returning to polite hostilities was so unbearable that she settled in her usual corner of the sofa to pour out.

'I would be unnatural,' said Rufus conversationally as he accepted his cup, 'if I had no misgivings at all on the subject, Jo.'

'What do you mean—misgivings?' asked Jo, frowning.

'Unusual though our marriage may be, Jocasta, I dislike the idea of my wife working in close conjunction with a man who was once her lover.'

Her eyes glittered with astonishment. 'Are you saying you're *jealous*, Rufus?'

He smiled sardonically. 'Is that so impossible to believe?'

'Yes,' she said baldly. 'It is. You and I don't have that kind of relationship.'

Rufus shrugged his broad shoulders. 'Whatever *kind* of relationship it is, Jo, it doesn't rule out jealousy on my part. I admit it's a new emotion for me. One you're never likely to experience where I'm concerned, of course.'

Jo drank down her coffee, got to her feet and locked glittering eyes with his. 'Mainly because it's pointless.

The only woman I need to be jealous of is dead, Rufus. Goodnight.'

It was deeply satisfying to sweep out of a room with a good exit line, but it was no help in getting to sleep. Jo spent most of the night tossing and turning, drinking tea at one stage, trying to read, but sleep was a long time in coming. And, having lain awake until the late grey dawn, Jo overslept. She got up to find the house empty and a note waiting for her on the kitchen table.

'You were asleep when I looked in. Don't work too hard. See you tonight. R.'

Not a note to tie up in pink ribbon, thought Jo morosely, and, after phone calls to her mother, Elizabeth and Susannah to report on her trip, made a start on the revisions Linus had mapped out with her. When Rufus came home he behaved as though their argument of the night before had never happened, and Jo co-operated, relieved. But after dinner, while they were watching a documentary on television, Rufus got up to answer the telephone, spoke briefly, handed the receiver over to her and strode from the room, his back more eloquent with disapproval than his face.

'Linus here, Jo. Sorry to interrupt your evening. How are the revisions going? Miles was on my case today, asking how soon you're likely to finish it.'

Jo reported on her progress, winning extravagant praise. 'Another week or so and I might well have cracked it. But I haven't come to the tricky bit yet—'

'Good, because I've thought of a new angle on the love affair. I'll play about with it a bit more tonight, then I'll ring you tomorrow.'

When Rufus returned, a glass of Scotch in his hand, one look at his face decided Jo against telling him the reason for Linus' call. This was unfair, she thought resentfully, staring at the television screen. Rufus had no right to behave like a possessive husband where she was concerned. Not when he was still grieving for Claire.

They watched the documentary to the end in silence. When it was over Rufus switched off the set and turned to her. 'Well? What did he want?'

Jo's eyes narrowed dangerously. 'If you mean Linus, he wanted to check my progress on the revisions. Miles Hay is breathing down his neck about it.'

'I trust Cole doesn't intend breathing down yours,' said Rufus, with a precision which drew Jo's attention to his glass.

'How many of those have you had?' she demanded.

Rufus gave her a hostile look. 'Unless I'm driving you in the car, my alcohol intake is nothing to do with you, little wife.'

Only Rufus could make the word 'wife' sound like an insult, thought Jo bitterly. 'How very true,' she said disdainfully, and got up. 'I'm going to bed. Goodnight.'

'Not so fast.' Rufus leapt to his feet, barring her way, his eyes gleaming with something Jo didn't care for at all. 'You haven't kissed me goodnight. Even a marriage like ours allows a chaste peck before bedtime.'

'You're in a foul mood tonight,' she said crossly. She reached up to kiss him on the cheek, but Rufus caught her in his arms and kissed her mouth, frustrating her attempts to push him away. His lips were cold from the ice in his glass, but his tongue was hot and conquering and Jo felt a streak of heat flash through her veins before Rufus released her so suddenly that she staggered.

'Go to bed,' he said harshly, and bent to pick up his glass. He toasted her mockingly. 'To married bliss, Jocasta.'

'You're a barrister, Rufus. If you don't like our marriage you know exactly how to end it,' she flung at him, and marched from the room, back straight and head high.

Next morning Jo took so long in the bathroom that Rufus was gone by the time she went downstairs, and this time there was no message on the kitchen table.

Jo took refuge in work, submerging herself in the alterations which, in some cases, were so much harder to get on screen than the original story. And because there was no Dolly that day to provide lunch Jo didn't bother with any and surfaced a little after two to the sound of the doorbell. She went downstairs irritably, flipping her braid over her shoulder, then stared in astonishment at the sight of Linus Cole on her doorstep. Or, more to the point, Rufus' doorstep, she thought with misgiving.

'I thought I'd surprise you. Had lunch on the train, of a sort, so I thought we could do some work together this afternoon.' Linus beamed at her, gave her a hug and a kiss, then held her away to look at her. 'You look about sixteen like that.'

Since Jo was wearing jeans and an elderly navy sweater and hadn't bothered with make-up that day, she felt irritated by the remark rather than flattered. 'You should have phoned, Linus. And don't tell me there isn't a mobile phone in that briefcase.'

'There is,' he admitted, 'but I fancied surprising you.' He looked around him in admiration as she led him through the house to the kitchen. 'I say, Jo, this is some abode. Your man loaded, is he?'

'No idea,' she said curtly. 'Want some coffee?'

'Please. Let's take it into your study, and drink while we work. Must catch the four-thirty train back.'

Since Jo's bedroom was her study, she had no alternative but to take Linus there.

'Fantastic bed,' he commented.

'Right, then,' she said briskly, hoping he wouldn't pick up on the lack of male occupation in the room, 'let's get on with it, Linus. But next time, ring first.'

When Rufus came home that night Jo, deliberately, was still in her jeans, face as nature made it and her hair straggling out in fronds from its braid. She'd been tempted to keep quiet about Linus Cole's unexpected visit, but in the end decided on her usual policy of honesty. But she wanted Rufus to see her as Linus had.

'Had a hard day?' he said in surprise as he came into the kitchen.

Normally Jo stopped work well in time to change and make herself as attractive as she possibly could, whether they were in a period of truce or not. Rufus looked effortlessly elegant whatever he wore, and Jo felt on her mettle at least to try to live up to him.

Tonight Rufus' surprise at her dishevelment was justified.

'I certainly have,' Jo said with feeling as she stirred the sauce she was making. 'I'm afraid the *cuisine* isn't very *haute* tonight. I got held up.' She turned to face him, a light of battle in her unembellished eyes. 'Linus Cole came here after lunch. Unexpectedly, before you jump to conclusions. He spent two hours here working on the book with me, then caught the train back to London.'

Rufus put down his briefcase, his face no more readable than it ever was. 'And was it a fruitful session?'

'I don't know,' she said frowning. 'He's got this different angle he thinks works better than mine.'

'It's your book. If you don't agree don't do it,' he advised, and leaned over her shoulder. 'What are we having?'

The subject of Linus, Jo realised with relief, was closed. Rufus said no more about him that evening, nor, indeed, about anything personal at all. And his goodnight kiss, thoughts of which had hung over her like the sword of Damocles all evening, was his usual salute on the cheek instead of the passionate, masterful embrace of the night before. Jo went disappointed to bed, but slept almost the moment her head touched the pillow, waking only when a knock on the door heralded Rufus' entry next morning to say goodbye.

'I'll be late tonight,' he informed her. 'Don't cook for me. I'm dining with clients. But cook for yourself,' Rufus added sternly, and to Jo's surprise he bent to kiss her cheek, trailed a long finger across it and strolled from the room.

Jo worked like a maniac, sometimes discarding the revisions she made, at other times pleased with her progress. Rufus was deeply disapproving when he discovered she intended to work right through the weekend.

'You look shattered, Jo—take a break. The forecast's good. We could drive somewhere for lunch on Sunday.'

Sorely tempted, Jo forced herself to turn the offer down. 'Just this one weekend. Then I can relax.'

He shrugged indifferently. 'As you wish.'

It wasn't at all what Jo wished, but now that the bit was between her teeth she was determined to finish the revisions by the following weekend as Miles Hay wanted. By Monday morning she felt she was winning. She was glued to her screen, concentrating fiercely, when the doorbell rang just after midday.

Dolly knocked on her door and popped her head round. 'There's a gentleman by the name of Cole downstairs, dear.'

Jo tore at her hair in despair. 'Oh, *no*, Dolly! Just as I was getting on so well.'

'He said he was your editor so I put him in the sitting room,' said Dolly apologetically. 'I was just going to bring you some soup and a sandwich. Shall I do some for Mr Cole, too?'

'Dolly, you're an angel!' Jo tidied her hair and slapped on some lipstick, then went down to greet Linus. 'You promised to ring first,' she said accusingly, and dodged the kiss he aimed at her mouth.

'You'd have told me to get lost,' he said, unabashed, 'and I've thought of a brilliant new ending—'

'Stop right there,' said Jo imperiously. 'I've gone with some of your suggestions because I can see how much they improve the story. But the ending is mine. I want it exactly the way it is. And if that means you don't want to publish it I'll take it somewhere else—'

'Hey! Slow down.' Linus gave her a conciliating hug.

'Cut it out, Linus,' she said irritably, and pushed him away. 'My wonderful Mrs Dalton has made us a snack lunch. We'll eat while we work.'

Linus accepted with enthusiasm. She wrangled with him as she'd never have done with the unknown Miles Hay, but in the end, with input from each of them, Jo felt satisfied that the finished result was good, and exactly as she wanted it, with her own original ending that Linus had the grace to admit worked better than his own idea.

'Right,' she said briskly. 'Give me a day or two to go through it all again to see the pieces fit, then I'll mail it to you.'

Linus stood up, stretching. 'We're a good team, Jo. When do I get the next one?'

Secretly delighted that Diadem wanted a follow-up, Jo shrugged nonchalantly. 'I've already started on it.'

'Good girl.' Linus stood looking at her for a moment, an oddly avuncular expression on his face. 'Who'd have thought it! Little Jo.'

Jo gave him a push. 'Don't get mushy, Linus. You'll miss your train.'

'True. Thank your lady for the lunch.' He threw his arms round her and kissed her affectionately.

'Am I interrupting?' enquired a cold, dispassionate voice, and Jo turned in dismay to see Rufus in the doorway.

'Not at all,' she said calmly. 'Rufus, this is my old college friend, Linus Cole. Linus, my husband, Rufus Grierson.'

The two men shook hands, Linus in no way put out at being interrupted mid-kiss with the wife of a man who was all too obviously enraged at the discovery. He congratulated Rufus on his clever wife, asked Jo to get the finished manuscript to him as soon as possible, then went downstairs with Rufus as a taxi arrived to take Linus to the station. Before the door had closed behind him Jo went into her room and shut the door, feeling sick with apprehension.

Jo took the coward's way out, and postponed the hour of confrontation by taking a bath, and afterwards dressed in something rather more prepossessing than the jogging pants and fleece-lined sweatshirt worn during the session with Linus. She went down to the kitchen to start preparing dinner at last, her jagged nerves well hidden behind the well-groomed mask she presented to her husband every night when he came home.

She turned from the pan she was stirring as Rufus strolled into the kitchen a few minutes later. 'You were home early today,' she said, carrying the war into the enemy's camp.

'Yes,' he said grimly. 'I apologise for my inopportune appearance.'

'No need,' she returned. 'Linus was just going.'

'Having received what he came for, no doubt!' His eyes smouldered into hers in a way she'd never seen before.

'Well, yes.' Jo swallowed. 'We more or less finished the revisions.'

'When? Before he took you to bed or afterwards?'

'What?' She stared at him, incensed. 'Are you mad?'

'I must be.' Rufus glared back, his eyes murderous. 'For starters, I assumed you worked down here, not in your bedroom. It's hardly surprising I felt "mad" when I found another man in a place where I am never invited.' He seized her by the wrist. 'But let's stick to the facts, Jocasta; I'm neither mad nor blind. I saw the bed. You hadn't bothered to straighten it. But then, I'm not usually home so early, am I? You thought you had plenty of time to conceal the evidence.'

Jo's eyes flashed. 'The bed was untidy,' she returned hotly, 'because we'd been sorting out pages of manuscript all over it. Linus and I are old friends, remember, so he kissed me goodbye as he was leaving. But we did *not* go to bed. Let me go,' she snapped. 'You're bruising my arm.'

Rufus dropped her wrist as though it burnt him. 'Are you asking me to believe that Cole spent several hours with you in your bedroom and never tried to make love to you?'

'Of course I am, because it's the truth. Why is it so hard to believe, Rufus?'

'Because he's a man, you idiot girl, *and* he was once your lover!'

They glared at each other, breathing hard, as though they were making love rather than war, then Jo's full mouth curved in a cold, mirthless little smile.

'It's amazing that a man who's supposed to be such a brilliant lawyer can be so utterly mistaken. Believe me, Rufus, I have a very good reason for not letting Linus Cole make love to me. Come on, you're the legal man. You should be asking what it is.'

'Is it another man?' he demanded, his eyes glittering darkly with a look that Jo had no idea how to interpret.

But then, when had she ever known what Rufus thought, or felt, except when it came to Claire? 'No way,' she said scornfully.

All the heat and anger drained from Rufus' face, leaving his eyes blank, as though a light had switched off behind them. 'No more guessing games, Jo. If you want to give your reasons, fine. If not, perhaps you'll excuse me. I'm going out.'

'Where?' she said involuntarily.

'I've no idea.' He gave her the smile she loathed. 'Does it matter?'

Jo breathed in deeply, and laid down the wooden spoon to prevent herself from hitting him with it. 'Before you go do me the courtesy of listening while I explain why even if I wanted to, which I don't, I could never let Linus—or any other man—make love to me. It's all your fault,' she added, eyes kindling.

Rufus eyed her narrowly. '*My* fault?'

'Oh, yes.' Jo folded her arms across her chest. 'I've never thought of myself as particularly vain, but I really don't fancy exposing myself to the kind of rejection you dished out at Christmas, Rufus Grierson.

You made it clear you require your women flawless. For all I know the rest of your sex feel the same way.'

Dark colour surged in Rufus' face, then receded so suddenly that his eyes burned darkly against his pallor. 'Flawless,' he repeated harshly. 'Is that what you thought?' He moved towards her, and Jo retreated, suddenly breathless.

'My scar,' she said unevenly. 'You were appalled by it.'

'I don't deny it,' he retorted, moving so close that Jo was backed up against a cupboard with nowhere to go. 'It did appal me. I hadn't seen it before, remember. It horrified me. But not because it was a *flaw*, woman.' He seized her by the shoulders, his eyes boring down into hers. 'That night, as you well know, I was desperate to make love to you. Then I saw the scar and I couldn't.'

'Because it revolted you,' Jo said dully.

He shook her a little. 'No. Not that. Think, darling.'

Darling? 'What must I think about?' she said wildly.

Rufus pulled her into his arms and held her close against his chest, his heart thudding against hers. 'I made you pregnant the first time I made love to you. Then I made love to you a second time and you were rushed to hospital and almost died. I swore I'd never touch you again unless I made certain you wouldn't suffer for it. But at Christmas when I held you in my arms I forgot everything except how much I loved and wanted you—'

'Loved?' said Jo, leaning back to look up at him.

Rufus frowned. 'Surely you knew!'

'How could I?' She glared at him. 'You forgot to mention it.'

'I was waiting for the right time to present itself— but to hell with that. Life's too short.' Rufus bent his head and kissed her fiercely and Jo responded with such fervour that it was some time before he raised his head, breathing hard. 'The scar, far from disgusting me, brought me to my senses, warned me not to put you in any such danger again.'

'Danger?' she said huskily, and wriggled closer.

Rufus breathed in sharply, and crushed her close, his face a hair's breadth away from hers. 'In our particular circumstances it was unlikely you were doing anything about contraception, Jocasta Grierson.'

Jo nodded. 'Very true.'

'Unfortunately at that stage neither was I. And no way was I going to get you pregnant again,' he said against her mouth.

'Oh.'

'Yes. Oh.'

They kissed each other with mounting passion, until something made Jo pull away a little to look up at him searchingly.

'Do you really love me, Rufus?'

To her dismay he drew away and thrust a hand through his crisp, silvered hair, eyeing her in a way which gave Jo deep misgivings. 'Look, I think it's time we brought everything out in the open, but let's do it in comfort, in front of the fire.'

'What about dinner?' she asked half-heartedly.

'Switch it off or throw it away,' he said sweepingly. 'I'll get something sent in later.'

Jo smiled crookedly. 'I'd only got as far as making some hollandaise sauce. I hadn't even defrosted the salmon fillets.'

'Ah. You intended softening me up by serving my favourite dinner!' he accused, and took her hand. 'I'll tell you a secret, Jocasta Grierson. There's a far easier way to do it. Remind me to show you how—later.'

Jo smiled radiantly, and let him take her hand to lead her into the sitting room, where the fire was now glowing in welcome.

Rufus closed the curtains while Jo switched on lamps, then he drew her down beside him on the sofa. 'I know you think of the sofa as your private domain, but not tonight. I need to hold you while I confess.'

Jo pushed her hair back behind her ears, and settled into the crook of his arm. 'Confess? What crime did you commit?'

Rufus breathed in very deeply, and tightened his arm around her. 'I think it's time you knew I fell in love with you the day I married Claire.'

Jo stiffened. *'What?'* she demanded, twisting round to look up at him. 'Are you serious?'

'Totally.' Rufus nodded gravely, smoothing a hand down her cheek. 'Fate played a hellish trick on me, didn't it? You know I met Claire at a hunt ball. She was beautiful and sweet, and we were soon seeing a lot of each other. But she wouldn't move in with me because her parents wouldn't have liked it. Nor, I suspect, would she. She was very conventional in some ways, and desperately keen to get married. I'd grown fond of her, and she made it plain she loved me. She wanted children and I found I liked the idea of a family a lot, so within months—the time it took for

Gloria Beaumont to organise the wedding of the year—we were married. But up to that point, for one reason and another, I had never actually met her wonderful friend Jo.'

'No,' said Jo, feeling as though her world had turned upside down. 'I heard you were gorgeous and successful and the most wonderful man in the universe, of course. But I was on holiday when the Beaumonts threw a party for your engagement, and you were working in London in those days. Claire went up there a lot to meet you, so somehow I never did. We almost met for lunch one day, when I went up to London with her for a fitting for my bridesmaid's dress.'

'But I was held up and by the time I got to the restaurant you'd gone,' he said wryly. 'I began to wonder if you really existed.'

'Unlike Claire I worked for a living. I had to catch a train to get back to the *Gazette*.' Jo looked down at the rings on her third finger. 'So we saw each other for the first time on the wedding day because I even missed the rehearsal. My boss sent me off to interview a local celebrity for the star feature spot.'

'I didn't see you at first when you came down the aisle,' said Rufus very quietly. 'Claire looked even taller than usual in all her bridal glory. You were hidden behind her.'

'I saw *you*,' whispered Jo.

'We came face to face for the first time in the vestry, during all the kissing.'

'You didn't kiss me.'

'Too damn right I didn't. I was afraid to touch you!' said Rufus with sudden violence. 'I couldn't believe it. Minutes before I'd made promises to Claire I could never break. Then I saw this little dark thing with flowers in her hair and fell head over heels in love for the first time in my life. But it was too late. I could hardly tell Claire I'd changed my mind.' He sighed heavily. 'Then or any time.'

'No,' agreed Jo sadly.

'Of course you made it easy for me, because you avoided me like the plague.' Rufus put a hand under her chin and raised her face to his. 'Why, darling? I assumed you took an instant dislike to me—so did Claire, because she stopped trying to bring us together after a while.'

Jo gave him a crooked little smile. 'Your wedding day was one of the worst of my entire life up to that point. Claire and I used to laugh over the book her mother bought on wedding etiquette. But it lacked a chapter on what the chief bridesmaid should do if she fell hopelessly in love with the bridegroom. Which I did. And to cover it I pretended to dislike him.' Her smile wavered. 'I thought that if I pretended hard enough it might become reality. But it didn't. I tried so hard, I even got engaged to someone else.'

Rufus stared at her for a moment, dumbfounded, then he hauled her onto his lap and kissed her with such passionate thanksgiving that Jo's eyelashes were spangled with tears when she opened them at last to a look she'd never seen in his dark eyes. They blazed with love. And, miraculously, it was all for her.

He rubbed his cheek against hers. 'Jo, I did my best to be a good husband to Claire.'

'I know you did. You made her very happy.' Jo shivered. 'I tried to be a good friend, too, but sometimes it was so *hard*. She talked about you all the time.'

'She talked about *you* all the time to me.' Rufus smiled crookedly. 'She even forced us to dance together once. At that party we gave for New Year's Eve.'

Jo shuddered. 'I remember. The music was slow and smoochy, and you held me away from you as if I had some infectious disease!'

He grinned. 'I was afraid to pull you close in case you blacked my eye when you found what you were doing to me.'

'Oh!' She giggled, burying her face against him. 'I thought you couldn't bear the sight of me. I think Claire thought that too.'

'It seemed the easiest way to deal with the situation.' Rufus sobered. 'Then she died and I felt so bloody guilty because everyone—including you—thought I was devastated. Which I was. But part of it was guilt because I hadn't been able to love Claire as she should have been loved.' He sat Jo upright, holding her by the shoulders. 'So then I was free. But by that stage, of course, you'd got yourself engaged to someone else. I didn't know you'd broken it off until just before that night.'

'The night of your anniversary.'

'The night I first made love to you.'

They looked at each other for a moment.

'Are you hungry?' asked Rufus casually.

'Not particularly.'

'Good.' He stood her on her feet, and got up to take her by the hand. 'I'm a lawyer, remember. You say you love me but I need proof. The physical kind.'

'I thought you were against that kind of thing in case I got pregnant again,' said Jo breathlessly as he made for the door, pulling her with him.

'You won't,' he assured her. 'After what happened at Christmas I'm now prepared against just such a contingency.'

'But I *want* another baby, Rufus,' she protested as he raced with her up the stairs to her room.

He picked her up and carried her to the beautiful bed. 'So do I. But not yet. I've only just discovered that the woman I love actually loves me. I want you to myself for a while, darling. Let's enjoy being married to each other before we get to be parents.' He stretched out beside her and drew her into his arms. 'I still can't believe this is all true.'

'Neither can I,' said Jo, and abandoned herself to the joy of kisses and caresses made all the more rapturous by the knowledge that they were the natural result of mutual love instead of mere physical chemistry.

Rufus undressed her slowly, savouring the task, kissing the places he uncovered. When he came to the scar, he pressed delicate kisses all along its length, until Jo could bear it no longer and instigated some caresses of her own which quickly brought about the inevitable, long desired result as they found rapturous fulfilment together after the long, cold weeks of estrangement.

'I dreamed about this, Rufus,' said Jo afterwards, when she could speak. 'I never believed it would really happen. When you insisted on marrying me I thought you were just doing the honourable thing.'

'Getting you pregnant was an unexpected short cut to being your husband,' said Rufus lazily, running a hand over her hip. 'If I hadn't I'd have wooed you until you gave in.'

'"Wooed"?' Jo chuckled. 'I like that word almost as much as "cosset".' She sobered. 'Poor Claire. I hope she never had an inkling of how we felt.'

'If neither of us suspected the other's feelings I'm certain Claire didn't. I did everything within my power to make her happy—and so did you.' Rufus rubbed his chin over her hair. 'We did our best in our separate ways to make sure she never knew. It wasn't her fault she was the wrong bride.'

'I thought *I* was,' said Jo. 'Mrs Beaumont certainly thought so. She told me only recently you'd never get over Claire and how nice it was that you had me to comfort you.'

Rufus scowled. 'She was the one who misled me about your engagement.'

Jo sat up to look down at him, pushing her hair back behind her ears. 'You don't think *she* knew how we felt?'

'No.' Rufus pulled her down to him. 'She just can't cope with the idea of Claire's husband happily married to someone else.'

'When did you find out I'd broken it off with Edward, then?'

'That night at the Mitre. I saw you behind the bar, and asked Phil Dexter if you were married.'

'He never said a word!'

'I asked him not to.'

Jo wriggled closer. 'Mrs Beaumont wasn't a bit interested when I told her about the book.'

'I am. *Deeply* interested,' he assured her, grinning. 'I remember what you said about being a kept man. The idea appeals—strongly!'

The following autumn Rufus Grierson came home one evening to a euphoric wife.

'What's all the excitement?' he demanded, kissing her.

Jo returned his kiss with enthusiasm, then dragged him by the hand into the dining room, and pointed to the small stack of hardback novels on the table. 'My book,' she announced, eyes shining. 'In good time for the Christmas sales.'

Rufus gave her a rib-cracking hug, then picked up the book, studying the jacket. An impressionist-type painting depicted two girls running barefoot towards a shadowy male figure on a deserted beach, with storm clouds massing on the horizon. He stared, arrested, and opened the book, gazing down at the page in silence. The title, *Storm Warning*, by Jocasta Grierson, was followed by the simple dedication 'For Claire'.

'Do you like it?' she demanded breathlessly. 'I wanted you to see it first before anyone else did.'

'It never occurred to me,' he said slowly, 'that you'd—'

'Dedicate it to Claire?'

'Not that—though it's a beautiful thought, darling. I was looking at the author's name,' he said, an odd catch in his voice.

'Oh.' She eyed him uncertainly. 'I never thought to ask. Would you have preferred me to use Fielding?'

'Absolutely not.' Rufus took her in his arms, hugging her close. 'Darling, I'm deeply honoured.'

'Well, I am your wife,' she pointed out.

He rubbed his cheek against her hair. 'And very happy I am with the arrangement. How about you?'

Jo hugged him close. 'You know I am.' She looked up at him, her eyes dancing. 'Now I know I'm not the wrong bride, I quite like being married to you, Rufus.'

'I'm not so sure I like the "quite" bit,' he said threateningly, and caught her by the hand. 'Let's go to bed. We can eat later.'

'Much later,' she agreed breathlessly as they went upstairs.

'If you're very good to me,' he informed her as they sank down together on their beautiful bed, 'I'll take you out to dinner. At the Chesterton, in honour of the occasion.'

Jo slid her arms round his neck. 'I've already booked. I got an advance from Diadem today—*I'm* buying dinner.'

'Are you now?' Rufus laughed, and held her tight, his lips to her throat. 'In that case I'd better be good to you, instead.'

'Better than *good*,' she ordered, smiling. 'Just be wonderful—as usual.'

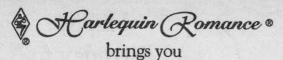

Harlequin Romance ®

brings you

BABY BOOM

We are proud to announce the latest arrival in our bouncing baby series— Baby Boom!

Each month in 1997 we'll be bringing you your very own bundle of joy—a cute, delightful romance by one of your favorite authors. Our heroes and heroines are about to discover that two's company and three (or four...or five) is a family!

This exciting series is all about the true labor of love...

Watch for:
#3453 FIRST-TIME FATHER
by Emma Richmond

She's a widow with a small baby. He's a dangerously sexy hunk who always gets what he wants. But he's reckoned without one adorable baby who has decided that this perfect bachelor would also make a perfect dad!

Available in April wherever Harlequin books are sold.

Happy Birthday to

Harlequin Romance®

It's party time....
This year is our
40th anniversary!

**Forty years of
bringing you the best
in romance fiction—and
the best just keeps
getting better!**

To celebrate, we're planning
three months of fun, and prizes.

Not to mention, of course,
some fabulous books...

The party starts in **April** with:

Betty Neels
Emma Richmond
Kate Denton
Barbara McMahon

Come join the party!

Heartbreak RANCH

Four generations of independent women…
Four heartwarming, romantic stories of the West…
Four incredible authors…

Fern Michaels
Jill Marie Landis
Dorsey Kelley
Chelley Kitzmiller

Saddle up with Heartbreak Ranch, an outstanding
Western collection that will take you on a whirlwind
trip through four generations and the exciting,
romantic adventures of four strong women who
have inherited the ranch from Bella Duprey,
famed Barbary Coast madam.

Available in March,
wherever Harlequin books are sold.

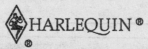

HARLEQUIN ®

HARLEQUIN®

Don't miss these Harlequin favorites by some of our most distinguished authors!
And now, you can receive a discount by ordering two or more titles!

HT#25645	THREE GROOMS AND A WIFE by JoAnn Ross	$3.25 U.S. ☐ $3.75 CAN. ☐
HT#25647	NOT THIS GUY by Glenda Sanders	$3.25 U.S. ☐ $3.75 CAN. ☐
HP#11725	THE WRONG KIND OF WIFE by Roberta Leigh	$3.25 U.S. ☐ $3.75 CAN. ☐
HP#11755	TIGER EYES by Robyn Donald	$3.25 U.S. ☐ $3.75 CAN. ☐
HR#03416	A WIFE IN WAITING by Jessica Steele	$3.25 U.S. ☐ $3.75 CAN. ☐
HR#03419	KIT AND THE COWBOY by Rebecca Winters	$3.25 U.S. ☐ $3.75 CAN. ☐
HS#70622	KIM & THE COWBOY by Margot Dalton	$3.50 U.S. ☐ $3.99 CAN. ☐
HS#70642	MONDAY'S CHILD by Janice Kaiser	$3.75 U.S. ☐ $4.25 CAN. ☐
HI#22342	BABY VS. THE BAR by M.J. Rodgers	$3.50 U.S. ☐ $3.99 CAN. ☐
HI#22382	SEE ME IN YOUR DREAMS by Patricia Rosemoor	$3.75 U.S. ☐ $4.25 CAN. ☐
HAR#16538	KISSED BY THE SEA by Rebecca Flanders	$3.50 U.S. ☐ $3.99 CAN. ☐
HAR#16603	MOMMY ON BOARD by Muriel Jensen	$3.50 U.S. ☐ $3.99 CAN. ☐
HH#28885	DESERT ROGUE by Erine Yorke	$4.50 U.S. ☐ $4.99 CAN. ☐
HH#28911	THE NORMAN'S HEART by Margaret Moore	$4.50 U.S. ☐ $4.99 CAN. ☐

(limited quantities available on certain titles)

	AMOUNT	$
DEDUCT:	10% DISCOUNT FOR 2+ BOOKS	$
ADD:	POSTAGE & HANDLING	$
	($1.00 for one book, 50¢ for each additional)	
	APPLICABLE TAXES*	$
	<u>TOTAL PAYABLE</u>	$
	(check or money order—please do not send cash)	

To order, complete this form and send it, along with a check or money order for the total above, payable to Harlequin Books, to: **In the U.S.:** 3010 Walden Avenue, P.O. Box 9047, Buffalo, NY 14269-9047; **In Canada:** P.O. Box 613, Fort Erie, Ontario, L2A 5X3.

Name: _____

Address: _____ City: _____

State/Prov.: _____ Zip/Postal Code: _____

*New York residents remit applicable sales taxes.
Canadian residents remit applicable GST and provincial taxes.
Look us up on-line at: http://www.romance.net

HBACK-JM4

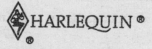

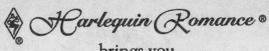

Harlequin Romance ®

brings you

SIMPLY THE BEST

Authors you'll treasure, books you'll want to keep!

Harlequin Romance books just keep getting better and better...and we're delighted to welcome you to our **Simply the Best** showcase for 1997, highlighting a special author each month!

Watch for:
#3451 ANGEL BRIDE
by Barbara McMahon

Angel had loved Jake but, without a word, he'd left. Now, two years later, Angel's life is at risk and Jake is back. But while Jake might protect her person, heaven knows what he'll do to her heart....

Available in April wherever Harlequin books are sold.